IN THE CUT

kevin bullock

IN THE CUT

Editor: Inkeditor Staff

Cover Design: Marion Design
www.meriondesigns.com

Book Layout: Shawna A. Grundy
sag@shawnagrundy.com

First printing March 2006

10 9 8 7 6 5 4 3 2 1

ISBN: 0-9717697-3-7

Acknowledgments

First of all, I would like to thank myself for waking from my mental slumber and finding my gift. Thank you, Ma (Jacqueline Wells) for loving me unconditionally for all of these years. I know it wasn't easy. You already know that if I got it, you got it. Thank you, May Kukulo, for being there for me. You possess a quality that's rare in women. I love you. To my sisters Katrina and Chevelle, I love y'all. To my uncle/father/brother, Robert "Spic" Bullock, you have played every role in my life except foe. I love you dearly.

To my sons Kevin, Dominic, and Kevin Jr., I'm doing this for y'all. And I have to thank James B. "Rico" Sims and the Inkeditor Staff for the terrific editing job they did on this book. At times, while I was writing it, Sims had me SO frustrated! But I knew that you were bringing out the best in me. And so what that everybody thinks you're arrogant; I feel you (smile). Last but not least, I want to acknowledge my peoples that know first-hand what the struggle is about: Curtis Barnette (I haven't forgotten about you); Keith "Wheat" Whitney (The Realest); Al Atwater; Clayton "Tree" Rand; L.D. Tory "Toe" Reid; The "Bright Twins"; Markeyo "short" McLendon; Chris Gilborne; Barry "Six" Williams; Leon Brady; Franciso Rubio; Jeff "Jazzy" Hyman; Mario Wright; and Emanuel "Ike" McCrae. While we are at our lowest, a lot of people have counted us out. A lot of people are glad that we are out of the way now so they can eat. But what we need to worry about is what we're going to do different this time to stay out. There are so many opportunities out there, and if we use the same energies that we put into the streets, we could conquer the world! I love y'all.

In memory of Jermaine "Puss Head" Ansley, Freddie Mack, Devondre "Boobie" Peace, Pee-Pee, Russel "Twin", DeAndre Caldwell, Elnora "Big Momma" Cozart, Shapeka Umstead, and Demetrius "Meatball" Owens.

If anybody wants to holla at me, my door is always open:
Kevin Bullock
P.O. Box 16042
Durham, NC 27701

PROLOGUE

Ten new inmates entered Dorm B and looked for their assigned cells. The whole dorm got quiet, trying to see if any of the newcomers were anyone that they knew. Brad sat in front of the TV and looked back at them. He overheard a group of guys sitting behind him.

"Aww, no the fuck it ain't!" said Thomas.

"What's that?" asked his friend.

"See that nigga right there with the long braids? That's the nigga who put my cousin Tory in a wheelchair."

"For real?"

"Hell yeah."

"What's up? I know you trying to punish that nigga."

"Hell yeah, I'm trained to go. Especially for my blood."

The four guys stood up, but Thomas thought of a better idea. "Hold up, let's wait 'til the yard opens. My cousin ain't gonna never walk again. I'mma stab this nigga." The men sat back down and watched the new guy walk to his cell.

Although Thomas and his crew were also from Durham, North Carolina, Brad had never so much as conversed with them. Their ways and actions told Brad from afar that it was best to stay away from them.

After a few minutes passed, Brad realized that he was no longer interested in the TV. He got up and headed to his cell. On his way, he was stopped by a man holding twelve boxes of oatmeal cakes.

"Yo, Brad. Here you go, homie."

"Goddamn, Pat. Why you ain't put them shits in your pillow-case?"

"'Cause I got to sleep on that shit. Here."

Brad grabbed the boxes and Pat walked away. When he got to

his closed door, he was about to set the boxes down so he could open them.

A newcomer said, "I got it for you."

"'Preciate it."

"No problem."

As the guy walked off, Brad sat the boxes down and came back to the door. "Hey!"

The guy came back. "What's up?"

"Where you from?"

"Durham."

"Me too. What part?"

"Over there by Walltown."

"Yeah? I'm from Bluefield," Brad said.

"My cousin stay over there."

"What's his name?"

"It's a her. Her name is Janice."

"You talking about light-skinned Janice that stay in the circle?"

"Yeah, that's her."

"Yeah, I know her. She wouldn't give me the time of day."

"I'm Manus."

"Brad." The men shook hands.

"So, how is this place? It got to be better than the joint that I just came from."

"It's a'ight. A lot of fake niggas. Especially from the homefront."

"I ain't surprised. I've been down six years. I been stopped that homie shit. Man respects man."

"You right." Brad smiled.

"All I do is stay to myself and out of the way."

Brad took an instant liking to Manus. "Yo, come in right quick and shut the door." Manus came into the cell and shut the door behind him.

"What's up?"

"Look, man. You seem like an a'ight dude, so let me put you up on game."

*   *   *

Thomas and his crew of three walked on the yard wearing coats in the seventy-degree weather. When they spotted Manus standing by the basketball court, they switched their direction toward him. When they were ten feet from him, Brad and four guys walked over from a nearby bench and stood beside Manus. They, too, were wearing coats.

Confused, Thomas looked at Brad, who stepped in front of Manus. "What's up, Brad?"

"Ain't nothing up. You tell me; I see you strapped. What's up?"

"Ain't nothing up with y'all, but that faggot-ass nigga right there … he shot and robbed my cousin."

"And?"

"And he got to answer for that."

"Ain't nothing wrong with that, but that's only between y'all two."

"What the fuck you got to do with it? What the fuck are you, a save-a-nigga officer?"

Pat stepped up. "My nigga ain't gonna be too many more names. Now, if you got a problem with this man, y'all can go in the bathroom and handle it however y'all like. But the rest of y'all niggas better stay out of it, or it's gonna be a massacre out here."

Thomas and his crew swallowed hard. They didn't want any part of Pat. He had a life sentence and was infamous for his knife work.

"Pat, what's up? I thought we were cool?" Thomas threw his hands up in a surrendering gesture.

"When it comes to my nigga Brad, I don't see nothing else."

Thomas looked at Brad then at Manus. He saw that Manus' face showed no trace of fear; he was calm and collected. Thomas judged him as a man of courage, a trait that he himself lacked. He said, "Y'all got it. I ain't trying to do nothing."

BOOK I – LIFELESS

I come in various sizes; I go by many names –
I give or take hearts from gangsters, or those who proclaim.
I act with no conscience; my actions usually burn –
I'll take you on a journey to the point of no return.
What am I?

From the book of *Flagrant Sorrows*
By: Kevin Bullock

The way she loves me, if it's a roller coaster ride then let it be –
She caresses my soul so good when we're up,
When we're down, the whole world is falling down on me.
She's the legs that keep me going; she's the air in which I breathe –
When she's down, I hear it in her voice, I dread the thought that she'll leave.
Her laughter is like a musical that relaxes and rids my stress –
With no patience I wait patiently through her face and stubbornness.
I love her.

CHAPTER 1

The sound of Brad's cell door being unlocked woke him instantly. But of all the times he'd heard the sound, today it sounded different. Today the sound was more profound.

The door was opened and Manus stuck his head in. "Get your ass up, nigga!"

"I'm up; I'm up."

"It's going down for the year two grand five. You getting out of this bitch."

"And they ain't got to worry about me no more," Brad said as he slid on his khakis.

After brushing his teeth and washing his face, they walked to the caferteria. They saw Pat sitting at a table by himself. He smiled when he saw the men. "Big day today, huh?"

"Yeah, man. I'm skating today," Brad said, feeling bad for Pat.

"All I'mma say is get out and do the right thing. A lot of us don't get second chances."

Brad nodded.

Pat said, "I see you nodding, but do you hear me?"

"I hear you."

"A'ight now. I catch you back here, I'mma knock you out and send you to P.C."

The men laughed.

"Well, I'm out," Pat said as he stood.

Brad stood also. "Take care."

"You too."

Pat walked away and Brad sat back down and faced Manus. "I tried to tell Pat yesterday that I wasn't gonna forget about him, but he wasn't trying to hear me."

"You know how it is; niggas be making so many broken promises before they get out. I guess he's just tired of that shit. You know?"

"But I'mma keep it real, though."

"Come on, now. You know I ain't doubting you."

"Word. But remember what I told you. I'mma turn you on to my connect as soon as you get out. If you keep it real with them niggas, you'll never have to worry about money again."

Manus sipped from a cup of orange juice. "That's what I'm talking about."

"I'm done, though. All I want is a good wifey, some kids, and a good paying job."

"You'll get it. All you got to do is stay focused, and don't fuck back with that broad."

"Man, I ain't going back to that broad. That's my good word."

"What if she's the first broad you come across?"

"I want some pussy, but I ain't stressed like that."

"I know you ain't. Especially with all them broads out there. The hell is one?"

"Know what I mean? I'm done with everything that's fast. I can't come back here. I'd rather die first."

"I feel you. Just stay low, and don't fuck—"

"I know, I know. Don't fuck with that broad."

"Exactly."

*   *   *

The bus ride home seemed to last forever. It gave Brad plenty of time to go over his plan that would keep him out of prison. He laughed about the misconception that most people had about prison: a place where a person got rehabilitated. He knew first-hand that prison only sharpens a criminal's tactics and hardens their hearts. He had chosen to give up crime because he could not handle being locked up again.

He had seen inmates suffer from neglect and betrayal from the outside world, and it had mentally scarred them and altered their way of thinking. He had also seen prisoners without a care in the world, living peacefully in prison. Prison had done a little bit of everything to him. It scarred him to the point where he didn't care anymore. And when he realized that he had gotten too comfortable, he bounced back to reality and got depressed all over again.

When he met Manus, they eventually became good friends. They discovered that they both were going through the same thing. Female problems.

Gloria, Brad's ex-girl, had crushed his world. Although they vowed to be together forever, she left him as soon as he caught three years for trafficking cocaine. It took a year for her to completely fade out of his life. During the course of that year, her letters and visits gradually faded. And although the truth was visible, Brad wanted solid confirmation. So when he received a one-page letter from her around Christmas, saying she couldn't do it anymore, it was a burden off Brad's shoulders. But at the same time, his greatest fear was confirmed. Manus had told him to be grateful for lessons like that. He said lessons like those were what made boys into men. Brad now knew this to be true.

Now as he rode home to Durham, North Carolina, Brad smiled because he was a man that had paid his dues. When the bus pulled up at the station, Brad immediately saw his mother.

Lauren had his back throughout the whole ordeal. She was a quiet woman who mostly kept her thoughts to herself. But, if asked her opinion, she would give it uncut. She was a woman in her mid-forties, in great shape. Her five-foot-ten body appeared athletic. Brad couldn't recall the last time he'd seen her eat junk food or meat.

Brad got off the bus and Lauren ran to meet him. She embraced him and said, "Baby!"

"Hey, Ma."

When she finally let him go, she said, "I'm so glad you're home out of that terrible place."

"Me too, Ma."

Watching the bus driver stare, Lauren said, "Let's get out of here before they change their minds or something."

On the way home, Brad admired the features and interior of the Mazda Millenium. Lauren noticed and said, "You like?"

"Like? Ma, this looks like a space ship compared to my old Regal."

"Oh, I forgot to tell you. Your Regal is gone."

"Gone? What happened to my Regal, Ma?"

Lauren let a few seconds pass before saying, "I traded it in and got you this."

"What? This is my car?"

"Yes. But not until you get your license renewed."

Brad leaned over and kissed her cheek. "Thank you, Ma. But how could you afford it?"

"My job pays me enough for the down payment and the first two payments. You're on your own after that."

"I got to find a job quick."

"I have a friend that's willing to give you a job."

"Yeah? Doing what?"

"Putting in wood floors."

"Yeah, I can do that. Thank you, Ma."

"You know I got to look out for my baby."

*   *   *

The next day, to Lauren's delight, Brad went to the DMV and renewed his driver license. When taking the test, he was distracted by women of all shapes and sizes that came and went.

What surprised him the most was that after all the reviving he had done to prevent being institutionalized, he had only broken the surface. This morning when he had gotten up, he went to the bathroom and put a "shit jacket" on the toilet. Then after that, he had sat and watched TV with his stomach growling until he realized that no one would call him for chow. Brad knew that eventually he would be back to normal; he just needed a little time to readjust.

When he returned from the DMV, he saw the woman that lived next door. She was struggling to take her groceries out of her car. Brad quickly got out of his car and went to help her.

"Let me give you a hand."

The woman took one look at Brad and smiled. "Thank you."

After Brad took the six bags of groceries in her house, she held out her hand. "I'm Kim."

He shook it. "Brad."

"I appreciate that very much. I must have looked so pitiful struggling with those bags."

Smiling from ear to ear, Brad said, "I wouldn't say pitiful. It's just my nature to be a gentleman."

The woman cocked her head slightly. "You must be from far away?"

"Actually I'm from here. I stay next door."

"With your wife?"

"No, with my mother."

"Oh. I haven't seen you around."

"Uh … I really just got back from sort of a vacation."

Understanding what he was saying, Kim said, "Oh. That explains the glow."

Brad's hands instantly went to his face. "I'm glowing?"

Kim laughed. "You know what I mean."

"Yeah, I was just kidding."

They had an awkward moment before Brad said, "Well, it was nice meeting you."

"Same here."

As he turned to leave, Kim said, "Brad."

Brad smiled and turned around. "What's up?"

"Being that you helped me with my groceries, maybe you'll let me return the favor by cooking you dinner tonight? That's if you don't have anything else planned."

"I do," he lied, "but how can I resist an invitation from a beautiful woman?"

Kim smiled.

"What time?" he asked.

"Say … sevenish?"

"Cool."

*   *   *

At the dinner table, Brad couldn't keep his eyes off Kim's cleavage.

Kim noticed and smiled. "Don't cut your finger off."

Brad averted his eyes to his plate, feeling somewhat embarrassed. "I apologize."

"Don't. I understand. You've been away."

Brad nodded.

Then she said, "If you don't mind, I want to ask you a question about prison."

"Go ahead; I don't mind."

"What is it like in there? I mean is it like the show *Oz?*"

"At times it can be, but mostly it's just like the streets. Just minus the females. But you got guys in there that substitute men for females."

Kim frowned. "Uggh!"

"I know."

"Just sitting here with you, I can't picture you like that."

Brad dropped his fork. "Like what?"

Kim laughed. "In prison, silly."

"Oh. But believe me, I didn't fit in. I stayed depressed."

"So what are you going to do to stay out of there?"

"Everything. My mom's friend is giving me a job putting in wood floors."

"I got my floor done at my old house. Those guys make good money."

"Yeah. I'm done with those streets. I don't have another bid in me."

"I'm glad to hear that. Most guys go in and out of prison for years before they finally learn that they can't beat the system."

"You're right."

Brad picked his fork up. "This steak is delicious."

"Thank you."

"So, tell me something about yourself."

"There's nothing much to tell. I'm a nurse. I'm single."

"Why?"

"Why am I a nurse?"

"Why are you single?"

"Because I haven't found the right man yet."

"What kind of man are you looking for?"

"I'm looking for a man that, first of all, doesn't lie."

"Okay, keep going."

"I want a man that likes to be intimate."

He started smiling.

"And not just sex. I want him to hold me while we're on the sofa watching TV. I want to be able to trust him. That's real important."

"I feel you on that."

"So, do you have someone?"

"Unfortunately, no."

"What kind of woman are you looking for?"

He stared at Kim. "I don't think that I have to look for anyone anymore."

*   *   *

At two in the morning, Brad let himself in the house. He saw the kitchen light on.

"Is that you, Brad?"

Walking in the kitchen, Brad said, "Yeah, it's me."

Lauren sat at the table in a nightgown drinking a glass of orange juice.

"You're up pretty late."

"I got thirsty."

Brad went to the refrigerator and grabbed the orange juice.

Lauren said, "I like Kim, she seems like a nice woman."

Not surprised that she knew, Brad said, "Yeah, she is."

Brad poured himself some juice and put the carton back in the refrigerator.

Lauren said, "Thank you."

"For what, Ma?"

"For doing like I asked you and going to renew your license."

"God, Ma. You talk like I'm just rebellious or something."

"Back in your younger days, I swear it seems that you purposely did the opposite of what I asked you."

"Nah, I wasn't like that. I just had to experience something you couldn't teach me. That's all."

Lauren sighed. "Well, I hope your experiencing stage is over. I can't take it if you go back to prison."

"Ma, you don't have to worry about that. I'm done. Prison isn't for me; I'm too cool."

They laughed. Lauren got up and put her empty glass in the dishwasher. "Well, let me get back to bed. I put the number of the man that's going to give you a job on your night stand. He said call him tomorrow morning."

"Thanks again, Ma."

Lauren kissed the top of Brad's head and went back to bed.

Brad sipped orange juice and thought about how good it felt to be free. He knew that there was no way he was going back to prison.

CHAPTER 2

Brad looked over at Meat and said, "Yeah, my nigga will be out soon. I know you'll dig him."

"What's his name? I probably know him."

"Manus."

"Nah, I don't think I know him. What, you met him in there?"

"Yeah, through some beef shit."

"What happened?"

"He had just gotten off the bus from Bunn, and I heard these crab-ass niggas from East Durham saying he was the one that shot their peoples. They was gonna shank the nigga. I didn't know dude or nothing, but I definitely didn't feel them other niggas. So I pulled his coat."

"Yeah? So what happened?"

"After we even shit up, them niggas ain't want to do nothing."

"Niggas be warring like that up in there?"

"Hell yeah, but not against each other...unless it was some serious shit that happened on the streets that can't be talked out."

The men rode in silence for a minute. Then Brad said, "What's the name of the club we're going to?"

"Da Premier."

"How is it?"

"Man, that shit be popping. You'll see."

"Word."

Meat pulled out a plastic bag. "You want one of these?"

"What's that?" Brad asked, frowning.

"X pills."

"Hell nah. I heard them shits be killing niggas."

"Nah, that be them niggas overdoing it. Take a half of one and you'll be straight."

"How them shits make you feel?"

"It depends. You got different kinds that have you feeling different ways. These right here have you emotional and hornier than a muthafucka. You can fuck all night on these."

"Yeah? Give me a half one. How long it take for it to kick in?"

"About twenty to thirty minutes."

Meat gave him a half pill and took the other half with two whole ones.

Brad said, "Goddamn, nigga! Don't you overdo it!"

"Man, I got this. Just keep your eyes on the road."

As Brad drove through the city, he noticed how small and raggedy it seemed. Trash clogged the gutters and infested the yards of homes. Young and old people roamed the streets with spaced-out looks on their faces. Nevertheless, clean or trashy, Brad felt good to be home.

Once the men were inside the club, they went straight to the bar. Meat, who had popped a couple of pills earlier, was already high. His cool and laid back demeanor made him every girl's favorite. He went through women like a chain smoker went through cigarettes. It was very rare for him to have sex with the same woman more than twice; it made him feel attached. He hated attachments. Some women accepted this, others destroyed his personal property and bad-mouthed him.

As soon as the men got comfortable at the bar, a crowd rushed Meat asking if he had any pills. Meat looked at Brad and said, "I'll be right back. Hold my seat down. You straight, right?"

"Oh yeah. I'm good."

Brad sipped his drink and watched the scene. He noticed how everything seemed to be in 3-D. Feeling strange and good at the same time, he braced himself for the unknown. He tried to relax some, but tensed up when he saw a guy do a double take at him and start walking in his direction.

The guy said, "Brad?"

Hesitantly, Brad said, "Yeah, what's up?"

"I thought that was you. What's the deal?"

"Uh, nothing."

"You don't even know who I am, do you?"

"Hell nah."

"It's Boo. We went to school together."

Brad studied Boo's face for a moment before he realized that it was DeAndre Caldwell. "Oh, shit! What's going on?"

"Nothing, man. Took you a minute to recognize me, didn't it?"

"Yean, man. It's been that long."

"I know, right? I just can't believe I'm here talking to you."

"Why you say that?"

"I thought you were dead."

"Nah," Brad said awkwardly. "I'm still here. Just been off the map for a minute."

"Well, it's good to see you. Be easy, man."

"You too."

Brad thought about what Boo had said. *I thought you were dead*. At times, during the course of his prison sentence, he'd felt as if he were dead.

Meat came back and sat down. "You a'ight? You're sweating like a Haitian."

Brad wiped his forehead and notice his hand dripping with sweat. Through clenched teeth he said, "It's hotter than a muthafucka in here."

"It is a lil' bit, but that's them..." Meat saw Brad staring at the floor. "What, you dropped something?"

"Nah, that shit is moving!"

"Goddamn! Don't start tripping and shit. Just relax and breathe easy. It's mind over matter."

Brad took his eyes off the liquid floor and started watching the movement around him. That's when he saw a familiar woman approaching.

Meat saw her, too, and said, "What the fuck you want?"

Gloria put a hand on her shapely hip and said, "Not you!"

"Wouldn't have you!"

"What the fuck ever!" Meat looked at Brad. "Holla if you need me; I'mma be at my post."

"Word."

Brad looked back to Gloria and let his eyes trail all over her body. Her thick hips openly invited him. The slits in her shirt revealed that she wasn't wearing a bra, and her breasts pointed at him as if defying gravity. Her pecan brown skin was flawless, and the Mac lip gloss seemed to illuminate her lips. The curves of her body appeared to be chiseled, and her walk was such that it sold sex from a distance.

"You ain't have to let nobody know that you were out."

"I've been too busy working. I ain't seen nobody," he said in a smooth voice.

"Uh-huh, I bet. So who you fucking with now?"

"Why?"

"Oh, don't act like that. I was just asking."

"Nah, I ain't tripping. Nobody really."

"So you trying to tell me you ain't had none since you touched down?"

"Nah, I ain't saying that. I just don't fuck with nobody on no relationship-type shit."

"So, in other words, you're just whoring around? Matter of fact, you don't even have to answer that. I see who you're with." Gloria observed him with a slight smirk on her face. "So you ain't gon' give me a hug or nothing?"

Brad stood up and hugged her. Her long-forgotten yet familiar scent filled his nostrils, and her body felt unusually warm on his. Without being able to control it, Brad felt his penis become rock hard.

Feeling him on her stomach, Gloria looked down and smiled. "I can tell them other bitches ain't got shit on me."

Feeling somewhat embarrassed, Brad sat back down. "So who you with?" he asked.

"Tasha."

"You still hang with her?"

"Uh-huh."

Brad turned his head when he realized that he was smiling. Remembering that she was the enemy, he pushed away from the bar and stood. "Well, I'mma holla at you." He walked off.

The club was so crowded that it was impossible to drink without elbowing somebody. Every time Brad turned around, somebody was shaking his hand and telling him how glad they were to see him. He wondered where they were when he was confined and depressed. To stop all of the handshaking, Brad bought two drinks at a time to occupy his hands.

When he finally caught up with Meat two hours later, the pill had long since kicked in.

As soon as Meat saw Brad, he started laughing. "Bruh, you better sit your ass down before you fall the fuck out."

"I'm kosher," Brad lied.

"What ole' girl talking about?"

"Who that?"

"Gloria."

"Not shit, being nosey. Wanted to know who I'm fucking with."

"She got some nerve."

"I know, right? Where you been? I went in the bathroom looking for you."

"Yeah? Nah, I was in the girl's bathroom."

"The girl's bathroom? The fuck you doing in there?"

"With them pills, it's bound to go down anywhere."

"Nigga, you wild."

"She was, too."

"She couldn't have been about shit, getting down in the bathroom of a club."

Meat shrugged.

After a few moments passed, Brad said, "Why you ain't come get me?"

Meat started laughing.

Then Brad said, "My shit has been hard since ole girl gave me a hug."

"I should've, but I ain't get nothing but some mouth."

"But some mouth? Damn, that's what I wanted. Shit, I ain't had none since I been out."

Meat frowned. "What! You ain't had no pussy yet?"

"Hell yeah! I'm talking about some mouth. The broad that I'm beating talking about she only gonna do that for her husband."

"I couldn't imagine," Meat said truthfully.

Brad grabbed his throat. "Why I'm so thirsty? I done drank about ten Coronas."

"It's them pills. They have you dehydrated like a muthafucka. Let's go get something to drink."

"They done quit selling alcohol now."

"Word? It's that late?"

Brad looked at his watch. "Two-thirty."

"Let's get up out of here before the fights and mace start. Niggas always act up when them hoes start choosing."

*   *   *

"Girl, you need to move here with me. It's a lot of job opportunities here."

"Right now, I can't see moving all the way to Seattle," Kim said on the phone. "Durham isn't that bad; the economy is growing at a rapid pace."

"But just a few months ago, you was saying how poor Durham was. You must have met a man."

Kim just started laughing. "Oh, Kia, I have!"

"I knew it! Tell me about him."

"He's a wonderful person that's been through some trials and tribulations, so he's really focused on being a better person and succeeding. And on top of all that, he's so fine!"

"I'm so happy for you."

"I'm happy for myself."

"You deserve it."

"Who are you telling?"

"So where is he now? You suppose to be putting it on him now."

"You know I'm going to. He's at the club with his friend right now."

"He's not a club hopper, is he?"

"No. He even asked me if he could he go."

"What? You better lock that in immediately."

"I know. I'm thinking about going down on him tonight."

"Why not? If he's as good as you say he is, then he earned it."

"You're right. I'm about to get the candles and chocolate syrup ready now."

"Handle your business, girl."

*   *   *

Meat and Brad were getting in the car when the window lowered in the car beside them.

"Come here, Meat," Tasha said.

After seeing who it was, Meat went over to the car. "What's up?"

"What's up for tonight?"

As if that was her cue, Gloria got out of the car and walked over to Brad's. Not bothering to wait until she was invited, she opened the door and got in.

Brad had his head on the headrest with his eyes closed. Assuming that Gloria was Meat, he said, "Ready?"

"All day."

Brad opened his eyes. "What the ...Where's Meat?"

"Over there talking to Tasha. What's up for tonight?"

"What do you mean, *what's up*?"

"You know, what are you about to do?"

"Not shit, probably go home."

"Oh. Can you take me home?"

"Why Tasha can't take you?"

"Because she trying to creep with Meat."

"Meat ain't fucking with..." The sound of someone tapping on his window made him spin around. He saw Meat motioning for him to get out. Brad got out. "What's up?"

"Peep, I'm trying to knock this broad off. But if you ain't trying to take ole' girl home, then fuck it."

Brad didn't want to mess up what Meat had going on. "Go handle that, rap. I'll drop her off."

"You sure?"

"Yeah, it ain't nothing."

"Good look. Can you drive? You look bent."

"Yeah, I'm good," he lied. "This fresh air is sobering me up."

"Word. Well, I'mma holla at you tomorrow. You got to work, right?"

"Nah, I'm off."

"Word. I'mma hit you up then."

The men bumped fists and got into the cars.

Brad saw Tasha hand Gloria her pocketbook and whisper something. Then the women started laughing. *Slick bitches*, Brad thought.

He smelled marijuana and noticed the blunt in Gloria's hand.

She saw the look on his face and said, "It's cool to smoke in here, right?"

"Just make sure you dump them ashes in the right place."

"I ain't gonna burn your shit."

"Where you stay at?"

Gloria passed him the blunt and said, "Strawberry Hills."

Brad hit the blunt twice and passed it back. He was already high, and he didn't want to overdo it. With both hands on the steering wheel, he sat up and focused on driving.

Gloria stopped smoking when she saw cars zooming past them, blaring their horns. She looked over at the speedometer and saw that they were only going thirty miles per hour. "Brad! What the hell is wrong with you? You better speed up before you get pulled."

Brad saw how slow he was going and said, "Damn. That X got me tripping."

"You rolling?"

"Rolling?" he asked, frowning.

"You know, high off ecstasy."

"Hell yeah. First and last time, too."

Gloria's mind started pacing. She knew all about the effects that the drug had on people. She took them herself from time to time. "You're going to fuck around and pass out. Pull over and let me drive before you kill us."

Brad complied and they switched seats.

As she drove, he stared at her and imagined that they had never broken up and that they were on a trip.

While incarcerated, he had had many such dreams. Just being in the car with her now seemed like a dream. Brad felt a lump forming in his throat. "Ree, why you do me like that?" he heard himself say.

Gloria thought about that for a moment. "It wasn't something I planned; it just happened like that."

"After all this time, that's all you can say?"

"What do you want me to say, Brad? Shit, I was so young then. I tried to be there for you, but all kinds of shit happened."

"You fucked a nigga up bad, Ree. I thought it was all about us."

"It was. It is. I swear I regret how that shit went down. If I could go back and change shit I would."

"But you can't."

"Exactly. But I can make up for it, though."

"You can't even begin to imagine the shit I went through. There were days when I couldn't even eat and just wanted to die." Brad felt tears running down his face and wiped them away.

"Brad, you got to look at my situation, too. I went crazy when you left me. I ain't know what to do."

"You act like I planned to get locked! If you fuck with a nigga like that and something fucked up happens, you suppose to ride with him. Regardless. All that 'being young' bullshit is an excuse. That was some sucker-ass shit, Ree. Plain and simple."

It was silent in the car. The only thing that could be heard was Gloria's sniffles. Brad just stared straight ahead, looking at nothing in particular. Tears ran down his face freely, but he ignored them. He was tired of wiping them.

When they finally reached her house, she pulled in the driveway behind a Chevy Malibu and killed the engine. She turned toward Brad and wiped his tears away. "Just listen to me, Brad. You don't have to agree or nothing."

She had his attention and continued. "I know I did some fucked up shit, and maybe we'll never be cool like that again. All I want you to know is I always loved you and still do. And I would do anything just to get back on good terms with you."

When he didn't respond she said, "Come on, Brad. Don't cut me back for something I did when I was a child. We both was living day for day back then. We wasn't thinking about no 'what ifs' and shit. Back then, my whole life revolved around you. So when you left, you took much more than your presence. You took my routine, my life."

Gloria broke down crying and put her head in his lap.

Brad started rubbing her back and said, "I forgive you, Ree."

Gloria cried even harder.

After calming down, she was rubbing feverishly at his crotch. When she felt that his penis was erect, Gloria unzipped his pants and took him in her mouth. She deep-throated him, and it sent chills through his whole body. Brad knew this was wrong, but he couldn't stop her if he wanted to.

CHAPTER 3

Brad called Gloria's cell phone for the fifth time in twenty minutes and got the voicemail. He didn't want anything in particular; he just wanted to hear sweet words to soothe him on his day off. He wasn't mad at her for not being available; he knew that she was probably tied up with something important. When the phone rang, he snatched it up on the first ring.

"Hello?"

A computerized voice said, "This is a collect call…"

Brad let the recording play through and accepted the call. "Yo."

"Ahh, what's the deal?" Manus asked.

"Not shit. What's up with you?"

"Same ole. Ready to get out of this muthafucka."

"Boy, I know you can't wait. You're going to trip; it's so different out here. And these broads, I aint seen but two skinny ones since I've been out. Everybody else is thick to death."

"Speaking of broads, you still fuck with ole girl?"

"Who, Kim?"

"Damn, how many you got?"

"One and a possible."

"What do you mean?"

"To be honest with you, I'm not even feeling Kim no more. She's cool, but my heart is somewhere else."

"Your heart? Don't tell me that you got a bad case of the tender dick."

"Nah." Brad laughed. "It's my old flame."

"Old flame? I know you aint talking about Gloria."

"Yeah, I ain't gonna front. I hit that the other night."

"You what?!" Manus nearly shouted over the phone.

"I hit ole girl the other night."

"Brad, what's really going on with you?"

"It just happened."

"But by fucking with that broad, you made it a'ight for her to do what she done to you."

"I know, but them pills had me —"

"For whatever reason you did it, that's on you. You're my mans, and I've always tried to tell you some good shit. But all I'mma say about Gloria is —"

A computerized voice announced that they had ten seconds before the phone would cut off. Brad said, "Call me right back."

"Man, I'm about to go eat. It's bird day. I'll catch up with you later on this week."

"Word. I just sent you and Pat off some dough."

"Word. Good look. I'll catch up with you."

"One."

*   *   *

Manus hung up the phone with disgust. He put his walkman in his locker and walked to the cafeteria. Once he got his tray, he saw Pat sitting alone at his usual table.

"What's going on?" Manus said, sitting down.

"Not shit. What's up with you?"

"Just got off the phone with Brad's crazy ass."

"What he talking about?"

"He said he sent some dough off."

"Yeah? *My nigga.* I'm glad that he's keeping his word."

Manus sprinkled some salt on his greens and said, "Not completely."

"What do you mean?"

"That nigga done fell weak for that broad again."

"Hell no! I ain't going for that shit. Not after all that shit he talked."

"It's real. That shit got me semi-hot."

"You know how niggas are; you just got to let them do them, and you got to do you. Brad is my nigga and all, but by fucking with that broad, after how she drug him, that shows you a lot about his character."

He thought about what Pat said and knew that he was right. Manus had his own objectives to focus on. And in order for him to fulfill his dream, he had to be stronger than any weakness he might have. Ever since he could remember, Manus wanted to run the city like his father had. He wanted the love and respect that people from all over had given his father.

Throughout his life, he had seen people sell themselves short by settling for something beneath them.

Like Brad, he had chased his dream of getting rich for six years by means of hustling. Manus didn't knock Brad for deciding to install wood floors, but that type of work wasn't for Manus. If anything, he would open up his own business installing wood floors.

There was no doubt in Manus' mind that he was going to run the city. And with Brad's connections, he couldn't fail. Manus counted the days that he had left in prison and knew that it was going to be the longest forty-five days of his life.

*   *   *

As Brad left the house to join Meat, Kim's door opened.

"Goddamn," he mumbled.

"Can I talk to you for a minute?"

Brad walked over. "What's up?"

"I'm not trying to stress you or anything, but why haven't I heard from you?"

"Because I've been busy."

"You could have at least called me the other night to tell me that you wasn't coming over. I had candles and everything set up for us."

"I apologize."

"I bet."

"Don't act like that. You know my job takes a toll on me."

"You seemed to have had plenty of energy that night because you sure didn't come home."

"Uh ... I got drunk and spent the night over my boy's —"

Kim put her hand over his mouth. "Please don't. You know how I feel about liars."

Brad stayed silent.

Then she said, with watery eyes, "This is all my fault."

"No, it's not."

"I should have given you a chance to get that wild streak out of you first before I asked you to get serious."

Not wanting to hurt her any further by admitting that he didn't want to see her anymore, he just dropped his head.

Kim lifted it back up. "I want you to do what you think you need to do, and when you get tired, hopefully I will still be available." She kissed him on the cheek and went back in the house.

* * *

Brad and Meat sat in the food gallery of South Pointe Mall and ate slices of Sbarro's pizza. Meat said, "What's up for tonight? You trying to hit Da Premier again?"

"Nah, I can't. I suppose to be chilling with ole girl tonight."

"Who that?"

"Gloria."

Meat was silent for a moment, then he said, "You know she fucks with a nigga named L? He buss his gun, too."

"Yeah, I know. She been broke up with him, though."

"That's what she say. They been fucking around for a minute. And I hear he be beating her ass."

"Well, all that shit is over with now. That's some bitch-ass shit anyway, fighting a broad. Fuck around and see that nigga."

Meat just looked at Brad like he was crazy. He didn't understand men that fell in love with the scandalous female species. It confused him to see men set themselves up for letdowns like that. *What in the hell has she done to him?* Meat thought. *Was her pussy that good? Mouth?*

Brad saw that Meat was in deep thought and said, "Say what's on your mind, nigga."

"It sounds like you're ready to go to war with that nigga over the same bitch that left you high and dry in prison."

Brad slammed his slice of pizza down. "First of all, don't be calling her no bitch! Second of all, I don't have a problem with dude. But if he jumps out there, I'mma lay his ass down."

Meat looked past Brad and said, "Speaking of the devil."

As soon as Brad turned around to look, L looked right at him and headed their way.

*   *   *

Gloria's vaginal muscles tightened around L's penis as he climaxed. L moaned and collapsed on her. As he lay there, Gloria repeatedly worked her muscle on L.

When he caught his breath, he rolled over and lit a half-smoked blunt.

Gloria started rubbing his chest and said, "Bay, I seen this banging-ass outfit at the mall that would look good on me. It only cost three hundred dollars."

L blew the smoke out and said, "Why don't you ask that nigga Brad to get it?" Gloria tensed up.

Ten seconds passed.

L said, "You ain't gonna say shit?"

"Bay, it ain't what you think. See, me and —"

In a quick motion, L pinned Gloria down with an elbow to her throat and put the blunt out on her thigh. Gloria screamed and desperately tried to break free, but L was strong even though he was slim. In a menacing tone he said, "I know all about you and that nigga the other night. I should kill your ass, but since I slipped, that's on me. I should have took your ass to Jersey with me like I started to."

Gloria had met L two years earlier at the club. His green eyes and expensive clothes had attracted her to him. It wasn't until six months later that she found out how violent he was. In a strange way, it stimulated her because she was a woman that demanded attention, and she loved how L put guys in check that came off on her wrong. Even though it was she whom he put in check most of the time, she loved it all the same.

L loosened his grip. "All that shit out your system, right?"

"Uhmm-hm."

"I ain't gon' hear about y'all creeping or hugging no more in the club, right?"

"Unh-unh."

"Good," he said, as he removed his elbow. "Now what store you seen that outfit in?"

*   *   *

L walked up to them and said, "What's up, Meat?"

"Not shit, you got it. What's up with you?"

"Chilling. Just want to holla at your mans for a minute, if you don't mind."

"That's up to him."

Brad shrugged.

Meat stood and said to Brad, "I'mma be over at Subway hollering at this chick."

"Word."

L sat down. "Look, Dick. I ain't gonna beat around the bush. I heard some shit about you and Gloria that ain't sit too well with me. But because I slipped, I'm willing to let that shit ride as long as it don't happen no more."

"Hold up, rap. What gives you the authority to say what does and doesn't happen between me and Ree?"

"Who the fuck is Ree?"

"Gloria."

L took a deep breath and exhaled. "Don't worry about all that. Just trust that you're playing with fire." L got up and walked away.

Brad pulled out his cell phone and called Gloria.

"Hello?"

"Yo, I just hollered at your boy."

"What he say?"

"Look. I don't know who he think he is, but he got the game all fucked up."

"What he do?"

"He ain't do shit, just ran his mouth. Talking about he gonna let what happened between us slide as long as it don't happen no more."

"I told him that we was back together and he went bananas. I think we should just chill for a minute."

"Hell nah. For what?"

"'Cause that nigga is crazy, and I ain't trying to start nothing between y'all."

"I don't see that nigga!"

"I know you don't, but you just got out and you don't need that shit."

"So you just gonna let that nigga keep you from being happy?"

"I'm just trying to keep the peace, Brad."

"By staying with that nigga?"

"No, Brad. I already told you I don't fuck with that nigga. Especially on no level like I fuck with you."

"I don't believe that shit. Ain't no way that nigga wilding like that and you ain't giving him no pussy."

"Come on now, you saw how tight I was. I ain't done nothing with that man, or nobody else, in about six months."

Brad thought about how hard it was to penetrate her and knew that she was telling the truth. Just the thought of having sex with her made his penis erect. "Yeah, I know. So what about tonight? I miss you like crazy."

"I can't. He might try to follow me or something."

Brad was silent.

"Hello?" she said.

"I'm here."

"So you mad now?"

"Don't ask me no dumb shit you already know the answer to."

Gloria sighed. "I don't know why you're mad. I love you, Brad. That's why I'm trying to keep the peace. I don't want nothing to happen to you."

"Who the fuck do you think that nigga is? Ain't ... Man, fuck it. I'mma holla."

"Don't act like that. I promise to see you before the weekend is over. Okay?" Silence.

"Hello?" Gloria said.

Brad was gone.

CHAPTER 4

Gloria hung the phone up and bit on her knuckle nervously. She prayed to God that his run-in with Brad didn't rile L up again. She didn't feel like arguing or fighting.

But her main concern was whether or not L was still going to buy the outfit that she wanted. Gloria knew that she had to secure the purchase, so she dialed L's cell number. On second thought, she ended the call. Gloria knew that if she called him right after his run-in with Brad, he would suspect that she had talked to Brad. That would definitely ruin her chances of getting the outfit.

She picked the phone back up and dialed Tasha's number; she had to talk to somebody.

"Hello?"

"What's up, girl?"

"Hey. I was just about to call you."

"What's up?"

"My aunt that stays in Greensboro is having a party tonight; you want to go?"

"I doubt if L will let me go; he's on another one of his sprees."

"What happened now?"

"Some kind of way he done found out about me and Brad."

"Oh shit! What he do to you?"

"He ain't touch me."

"What?"

"Nah, girl. He just made me promise that I wouldn't do it again."

"Girl..."

"But check this out," she said, cutting Tasha off, "I sent him to the mall to get that outfit we seen and guess who he ran into?"

"Brad?"

"Uhm-hmm."

"He ain't do nothing to that boy, did he?"

"Brad said they just talked, but you know L."

"I know. He might try to catch Brad slipping and do something to him."

"That's what I'm scared of, so I told Brad that we got to chill for a little while."

"You better leave him alone permanently if you don't want nothing to happen to him. Or better yet, you need to leave L alone. He's stupid."

Ignoring the comment, Gloria said, "But I don't think that L is going to mess with Brad. Because if he was, he would have done it when he seen him. Remember how he done Ron at the fair when he found out about us."

Tasha shook her head. She loved her friend, but sometimes she just wondered about her. "So you not gonna come with me to the party?"

"I don't know; I doubt it. I'll call you if I'm coming."

"A'ight, bye."

*   *   *

Brad took his eyes off the road. "I still can't get over dude acting like he's a certified guerrilla or something."

Meat said, "Brad, let that shit go. We're about to hit the club where there are plenty of broads that won't say no. Forget about Gloria; that bit — broad ain't nothing but trouble. Y'all niggas gonna fuck around and kill each other over her, and the one that survives is going to jail. And you already know first-hand that she ain't gonna ride with you if you murk him. She couldn't even troop with you for them lil' three years, so imagine a body sentence."

Brad nodded.

Then Meat added, "C'mon, my nigga. I know you're smarter than that."

After a few moments of silence, Brad said, "You're dead-ass right. I don't know what the fuck I was thinking about."

"It's gravy, man."

"No, it ain't. Punch me in the face if I ever pull some shit like that again." Brad banged a fist with Meat's and said, "I feel like getting fucked up now. Where them pills at?"

"I got them."

"Let me get a whole one."

Meat was hesitant to give him a pill because he knew how they enhanced a person's mood. But against his better judgment, he gave Brad a whole one.

*   *   *

Later on that night, L and his two friends, Tee and Rome, sat in his living room smoking blunts.

L looked at Rome. "You got some of them Ed Cotas on you?"

Rome pulled out a capful of light blue number five percocets and tossed them to L.

He shook out two of them and tossed them back to Rome.

Rome said to Tee, "You want some of these?"

"Hell nah! They be having me nodding and some more shit."

Rome said to L, "Finish telling us about ole boy at the mall."

"Oh. But, yeah, I seen that nigga at South Pointe in the food gallery and ran up on him. You should've seen how shook he was."

Tee said, "Did you have the burns on you?"

"Yeah, my palm .40, but I really wasn't trying to do nothing in there."

Rome said, "Hell nah. That's straight-to-jail action."

"But anyway, I told the nigga that whatever he had going on with Gloria was dead."

"What he say?"

L frowned. "What he *say*? That nigga aint crazy. He ain't say shit, nodding like a baby."

Rome said, "I know that nigga from school. He's mashed potatoes."

Tee stood and stretched. "Arrggh! I'm getting dead lazy up in this muthafucka. What's taking your girl so long? I'm ready to hit the club."

"She is taking a long time." L walked to the bottom of the stairs. "Hey, Gloria! Hurry up. We about to roll out!"

A distant voice said, "Here I come!"

L patted his back pockets. "Where I put my burner?"

Tee said, "You don't even need it; we got some big shit in the car."

L saw Rome's smile and said, "Real talk."

*   *   *

The club was packed as usual. While Meat was at his regular post, Brad sat at the bar and consumed shot after shot of Crown Royal. Everything was going smoothly until he saw Gloria walk in with L and two other guys.

Brad felt a pang of jealousy, but quickly replaced it with hatred. He summoned up all the old hurt that he had experienced when Gloria first left him. Then he thought about how L had insulted him at the mall. Then he thought about the conversation that he had had with Meat. He brushed the hatred off. He knew that everything was going to be just fine as long as they gave him his space.

*   *   *

Tee leaned in close to L and said, "Look at that crab-ass nigga over there grilling us."

L looked in the same direction and saw Brad. Returning his stare, L said to Tee and Rome, "He got something on his mind, don't he?"

Rome said, "Let's go find out what."

Gloria grabbed L's arm. "Please, bay. Let's just have a good time. That nigga is just miserable. Don't do him no favors by killing him. That's what he wants."

L thought about that and said, "Yeah, you're right. I'mma let that nigga suffer." L then gave Gloria a long kiss. Then they walked to the opposite side of the bar.

Meat came from his post and said, "You seen what I seen?"

"Yeah, I seen them." Then he grabbed Meat by the shoulders and said, "Man, I don't know what I was thinking about. I screamed on you for calling a slut a bitch."

"It ain't nothing; we live to learn. But peep," Meat said, moving on to other things. "See those two broads right there in all white?"

Brad saw them. "Yeah, what about them?"

"I'm hitting the short one tonight, and her friend is trying to see you. You with that?"

"Hell yeah, I'll knock her down."

"It's a done deal then."

Brad stared into Meat's eyes and said, "Yo, I love you. That's my word. I'll crush any nigga that fucks with you."

Meat laughed. "Nigga, you fucked up, ain't you?"

"Why I got to be fucked up to tell my nigga I love him?"

"You right," Meat said, knowing that the pills played a big part in Brad's emotional outburst. "You good, though?"

"Yeah, I feel great. I'm floating."

"I know, nigga. You —"

Brad abruptly stood up. "Hold my seat down. I got to use the bathroom."

"I got you."

Brad walked to the restroom but, right when he was about to go in, Gloria came out of the women's restroom and saw him.

"Brad."

He turned around and frowned when he saw her. "What?"

She walked to him. "Don't act like that."

"What the fuck ever."

"Why you hang up on me?"

"'Cause I'm done."

Ignoring the comment, she said, "We can get up tomorrow, a'ight?"

"I wish the fuck I would."

"Why you say that?"

"I already told you, I ain't fucking with you no more. I'm done."

Gloria was shocked. She wasn't used to being rejected. "Brad, you don't mean that."

"*Shit.* I don't know what the fuck I was thinking about when I fucked back with you. I straight up played myself."

"I know you ain't mad about me being here with L. I told you I don't fuck with him like that."

"Bitch, you fucking him!" he exploded. "Probably both of us in the same day. You might as well get us together and let us run a train on your nasty ass!" With that off of his chest, he turned to walk off.

Gloria grabbed his arm.

Brad snatched away from her with so much force that Gloria lost her balance and fell on the smutty floor. Not bothering to look back, he continued toward the restroom. Gloria got up from the floor and looked down at her ruined outfit. When she saw some females smirking at her, she ran straight to where L was standing.

Before she could say anything, he saw how dirty she was and said, "What the fuck happened to you?"

"That punk-ass nigga slammed me just because I wouldn't talk to him!"

"Who, Brad?"

After nodding, Gloria buried her face in L's chest and began to cry.

L looked at Tee and Rome. "Let's go."

*   *   *

Brad sat down next to Meat, who was talking to a female.

"I can't tonight," Meat was saying. "I'mma try to see you tomorrow."

The jet-black woman folded her arms across her breasts and said, "Why we can't get up tonight?"

"'Cause —"

"I know you ain't brushing me off for that hooker in the white," she said, cutting him off. "I seen her all up in your face."

"Hold up, Kel. Quit acting like you my girl or something. We suppose to be on another level. Damn all that arguing and shit."

"But..."

"Let me find out you were fronting about being secure about yours."

Kel started smiling. "Boy, you know I'm just playing. So, tomorrow, right?"

"Definitely."

"Well, can I get a hug or something 'til then?"

Meat stood and gave her a hug. In the process, he tasted her ear and felt her shiver.

After she was gone, he turned to Brad. "What's up? You look heated."

"Nah, that bitch Gloria just tried to holla at me and I amped."

"You whipped her ass?"

"Nah, I told that bitch to burn it up."

Meat was proud of him. "That's what I'm talking about. Rick James them hoes. Love them and leave them."

The men had stayed in the club until it closed. To Meat's surprise, no fights broke out. He guessed that the men had gotten the females they wanted.

Once they were in the car, a black GS with dark tinted windows pulled up beside them. Neither man noticed it as a passenger window rolled down. Out of Brad's peripheral view he saw a figure come out of the window and point something at them. Brad instantly ducked down. "Oh shit!"

Following suit, Meat ducked also. Instead of gunshots, the men heard two females laughing. Meat peeped up and saw Tip, the woman in white, hanging out of the window with a cell phone in her hand. After her laughter subsided, she said, "Y'all was slipping. I would've had y'all."

The driver of the GS, Sabrina, said, "Did you see them? They were scared to death."

Meat said, "Y'all got us, but it's on now. I'mma get your ass for that."

A strange smirk came across her face. "You can't get it sitting there." The GS pulled off.

When Brad just sat there, Meat said, "Man, follow them. Oww, I'mma dog that pussy."

Behind the GS, Meat looked over at Brad and saw a funny expression on his face. "You straight?"

Brad exhaled. "Man, that bitch scared the fuck out of me. My heart's beating faster than a muthafucka."

"Just take some deep breaths; it'll calm down. Them pills be having your shit like that." Brad concentrated on his breathing until his heartbeat was normal.

On the highway, Brad said, "Where you meet them broads at?"

"At Tip's nail shop."

"The hell you doing at a nail shop, tricking?"

"Nah, I was getting a manicure." When he saw how Brad looked at him he said, "Yeah, I get manicures. You better start learning how to treat yourself. Them hoes be loving a nigga that take care of his self. Matter of fact, that's where I meet a lot of broads that I be beating."

"At Tip's shop?"

"Nah, I be switching up."

"I was about to *say*. That's..." Brad paused when he saw a car behind them with no headlights. Before he could react or warn Meat, the car pulled up beside them.

A fully loaded automatic Mac-11 began firing.

The bullets struck both men. The Millennium spun out of control and crashed into a concrete median.

As the car passed the GS, the Mac-11 spit its remaining bullets at it ...

CHAPTER 5

"**M**a ... Ma. I'm sorry," Brad said as he rocked in the chair that sat by the window.

Lauren stood in the doorway of the unfamiliar room and sensed that something wasn't quite right. "For what, baby? What's wrong?"

"I went back on my word, Ma. Now look at me."

Lauren walked toward her son. "Baby, what are you talking about? I'm confused."

"I'm okay, though. I just wanted to tell you to be strong."

Lauren, who was now crying, said, "Son, you're scaring me. Please tell me what's wrong."

"I'm sorry, Ma," Brad said, sounding distant. The more steps Lauren took toward him, the more the gap between them remained the same.

The phone rang.

Lauren woke up from her dream. She wiped the tears from her face and answered it. "Hello?"

"This is the Durham Police Department." Is this the residence of Lauren Taylor?"

"Yes, this is she."

"Are you the owner of a green 2000 Mazda Millennium?"

Lauren broke down crying. "Please tell me he's okay."

"I'm sorry, ma'am, but we need you to come to the Durham Regional Hospital."

*   *   *

The banging at her door woke Kim out of her sleep. When she saw what time it was, she swung her feet out of the bed and prepared to curse Brad out. He was the only person who would be knocking on her door at this time of night.

"This fool is crazy if he thinks he is going to have his cake and eat it, too." Kim reached the front door and peeped out the window. When she saw Lauren pacing on the porch, she quickly opened the door. "Hey, Lauren. What's wrong?"

Lauren opened her mouth to speak but only let out a high-pitched shriek.

Kim grabbed her. "What's wrong? Where's Brad?"

"They ... they told me to come to the hospital."

"Who?"

"The police."

Now Kim began to cry. "What happened? Is he alright?"

"I don't know."

"We gotta go see!" Kim ran to her bedroom and quickly changed clothes.

The women rode to the hospital in silence. Occasionally, a prayer from one woman could be heard. Still thinking about the dream she'd had, Lauren couldn't help but think the worst. The more she thought about it, the more tears ran down her face.

Kim blamed herself for leaving Brad on the porch like she did. She knew that she could have convinced him to stay at home with her if she had really tried. She promised God that she would quit cursing and go to church everyday if he spared Brad's life.

When they walked in the Emergency Room and asked about Brad, the receptionist directed them to a uniformed officer and a detective.

They walked over and Lauren said, "I'm Lauren Taylor. Is my son alright?"

The detective introduced himself and then said, "We're not sure, Mrs. Taylor. We have two men that were shot."

Both women screamed, "Shot!"

"Yes, ma'am. One of the men passed, and one is in surgery."

"Well, let's go see. I have to know right now."

The detective and the uniformed officer led the women to the hospital's morgue. As the women entered the room, the temperature seemed to drop twenty degrees.

Kim noticed that Lauren was about to have a nervous break-down, so she held her up.

The detective pulled out a cold slab to reveal a covered body. Blood stains at the head area could be seen on the sheets.

Both women felt nauseous.

The detective looked at the women.

Both women nodded.

The detective pulled back the sheet.

*　　　*　　　*

Manus was sitting at a table playing poker when Pat tapped him on the shoulder. "What's up, Pat?"

Pat sighed. "Let me holla at you."

From the look on Pat's face, Manus knew that something serious was going on. He folded his hand and got up from the table. "What's the deal?"

"I just heard some crazy shit."

"What's that?"

"That Brad got murked last night."

Manus started laughing. "Hell nah. Who told you some crazy shit like that?"

"My sister. She said the police had the highway blocked off."

"Nah, that can't be real. I just hollered at him last night. He sent us some money off."

"Man, call that nigga and make sure he's a'ight."

"I'mma do that right now."

As Manus was dialing Brad's number, he noticed his hands shaking. The phone rang six times before someone answered. After the call was accepted, a man said, "Hello?"

"May I speak to Brad?"

The man hesitated before saying, "Who is this?"

"This is Manus."

"Hold on, Manson."

Before Manus could correct him, he heard the man put the phone down. He was relieved to know that Brad was alright. He knew how the streets twisted stories up. If anything, Brad had probably just wrecked his car on the highway. In the background, Manus heard a lot of people talking. Then Lauren got on the phone sounding very distraught. "Who is this?"

"This is Manus, Ms. Lauren. How are you doing?"

"Oh, Manus. Nothing, just trying to make it, that's all."

Trying to make it? Manus thought. Then he said, "Ms. Lauren, where's Brad? I just heard a crazy rumor. Please tell me it ain't true." There was a moment of silence. Manus thought they had been disconnected.

Then Lauren said in a high-pitched voice, "It's true, Manus! They killed my baby!"

"No, man! Who?"

"Don't nobody know," she was sobbing.

"How did it happen?"

"Somebody shot him and his friends after they left the club. A girl died, too. His friend Meat and another girl survived."

"This can't be real!"

"They took my baby, Manus! Oh my God..."

Manus heard the phone drop.

Then the same man that had answered the phone picked it up. "Hello?"

"Is she a'ight?"

"No, man. She just needs some time to grieve. Thanks for calling."

Manus slammed the phone down and leaned on the wall. The noise caught the attention of the other inmates in the dorm, but they didn't think too much of it. It was common to see a grown man in despair after getting off the phone. Manus stood there and grieved for his friend. He felt like a part of him had been murdered as well.

Pat walked in the dorm. He studied Manus, then sighed. He walked up to Manus and the men embraced.

Manus said, "It's gravy. I'mma straighten it."

*   *   *

Two weeks had passed since the shooting. Meat lay in the hospital bed in a daze. One of his legs had been fractured in the crash. His head was bandaged because a bullet had penetrated the upper part of his skull. It had barely missed his brain. When Tip rolled herself into the room, he didn't notice her until she called his name. During the shooting, a bullet had ripped through her shoulder and had hit a lung. She wasn't paralyzed, but she wasn't able to walk because her lung had collapsed, causing her wind to be short. They, too, had lost control of the GS and crashed. Brad and Sabrina had taken direct shots to the head and died instantly.

Meat observed that even on her bad days Tip was still beautiful. Her natural wavy hair was pulled back, revealing her glowing brown face. Meat always thought she looked like Jennifer Freeman.

Finally she said, "What went on with y'all that night?"

It was a question that the police and Lauren had asked him a thousand times. A question he had asked himself a million times. Each time, he only came up with one scenario that made sense. A scenario that put him in a predicament. One that made him obliged to get healthy and take revenge. He only said to Tip, "Nothing that I know of."

"Y'all ain't argue with nobody or nothing?"

"Nah, we were chilling." His eyes shifted toward the window, away from Tip.

*　　　*　　　*

During the month that Meat was hospitalized, he received visits from over thirty females. Many of them came while another female was already there. It occasionally resulted in an argument, or a catfight. Some of the incidents occurred in the presence of Tip. When they did, she just wheeled herself back to her room.

*　　　*　　　*

Tasha sat in the living room of Gloria's house wiping the tears from her face.

"Quit crying, girl," Gloria consoled her. "He's not worth it."

"I can't believe how he handled me. That bitch wasn't even prettier than me!"

"You know how Meat is; he's a straight up dog. If I was you, I would have knocked his ass out of that hospital bed."

Tasha laughed.

"Yeah, girl," Gloria said, "don't worry about Meat. You're pretty and smart; that's his loss."

Tasha wiped the tears again and said, "You're right, it's his loss." She smacked her crotch. "He'll never get none of this no more! And that's on everything."

After a few moments passed, Tasha said, "let me ask you something."

"Go 'head."

"Did you love Brad?"

"I think I did."

"Then how come you never grieved over his death?"

"To be real with you, when he was in prison it was just like he was dead, because he couldn't do nothing for me. So, basically, it's the same way."

Tasha stared at her friend and realized for the first time how cold-blooded she was. She couldn't believe she hadn't noticed it before.

They heard a key being inserted in the door.

L, Tee, and Rome came in laughing. "What's going on?" L asked the women then kissed Gloria. Tasha took one look at L and instantly thought about how pitiful Meat looked lying in the hospital. She burst out crying and ran to the bathroom.

"What the fuck wrong with her?" L asked Gloria.

"Her and her boyfriend broke up."

*   *   *

On the day that Meat was discharged, he was surprised to see that Tip was there to take him home. "I told your Mom that I would come get you."

"When did you get out of that wheelchair?"

"About a week ago. I got my wind up."

"And you driving already?"

"Uhm-hmm."

Meat playfully rolled his eyes upward. "God help me."

When they arrived at Meat's apartment, the phone was ringing off the hook with women that wanted to come over. Meat declined them all.

Tip said, "Don't let me stop you from doing your thing."

"You ain't. I'm good with you here."

"Yeah?" She asked, blushing.

"Come here."

Tip walked over to him and he kissed her. Tip kissed him back, but when he began to unbuckle her belt, she stopped him.

"Come on now," he whined. "I ain't had none in a minute."

She grabbed his hands. "What do you want out of life? Are you just gonna play the field all of your life?"

"Why you all of a sudden getting complicated and shit?"

"As if it isn't the time."

Meat pulled his hands free from her grasp.

"Meat, we almost got killed over God knows what. Both of our friends are gone. My best friend!" Tears flooded her eyes and all of the built-up pressure and stress spilled out.

Meat just looked at her with mixed emotions. He understood where she was coming from, but he didn't know what to say. He didn't think her tears were staged, but he couldn't understand why she was there, or what she wanted from him. He picked up the phone and called Susan.

*　　　*　　　*

Brian Anderson lay in his bed listening to the phone ring. He hadn't answered it in a month because of the constant aggravation from the bill collectors. The last two years of his life had been hell. Now he knew the real meaning of a mid-life crisis.

It had all started when the police raided his pawnshop and arrested him for fencing stolen goods. Not too long after that, his second wife, who was twenty years younger than him, saw that the good life was over, and so she left him. Three days later, she filed for divorce. Her lawyer told him that his client was seeking the house. Brian was furious. She wanted the house that he had built from the ground up. On top of that, the police made it their business to post up in front of his shop during business hours. Brian knew that there was no way that he could continue the trade that had been so profitable without going back to jail.

Now, two years later, he lay cooped up in a one-bedroom apartment with only five hundred dollars to his name, the last of the money left from selling his pawnshop. His will was broken. To get back all he had lost would take lots of energy that he did not have. For the first time in his life he felt old.

Brian got out of bed to use the bathroom, and he heard a knock on the door. He wondered which bill collector it was. Ignoring it all the same, he went on about his business. After flushing, a head appeared at the window, startling him.

Bobby screamed through the window, "If you don't come and open that door, I'mma kick it down!"

"A'ight, a'ight. Go on around to the front."

The door was opened. Bobby said, "You damn fool! What in the hell is wrong with you? Won't answer your phone or the door. You got everybody thinking you're dead, too ..."

While Bobby continued the tongue-lashing, Brian tried to figure out what he was talking about. When it finally dawned on him, he cut him off. "You said 'dead, too'. Who's dead?"

Bobby just looked at his twin brother with disgust. His son had been dead for a whole month, and he didn't have a clue. Bobby sympathized with Lauren, the woman whom he still loved, the woman his brother had stolen.

Bobby had met Lauren when they were only seventeen. They had been dating for two weeks when Brian came to him in despair one night. He told Bobby that he had done the forbidden. He had slept with Lauren, and he was in love with her. Bobby was stunned. It was not uncommon for the twins to swap girls with the exception of the ones that they really liked. Lauren was an exception. What really crushed Bobby's heart later on was when Brian told him that Lauren was pregnant. The whole situation was convenient for Brian because Lauren only knew Bobby as "Twin", and to her knowledge, Brian was the only twin she had met.

It took him years to forgive Brian, but with Lauren, he had never quite gotten over her. In the ten years that Lauren and Brian were together, Bobby witnessed his brother take her through hell. During the rare moments that Bobby was around Lauren, her presence overwhelmed him to the point that he had to get away from her.

Bobby looked at his brother and said, "Brian, Brad was killed a month ago. He was murdered."

Dumbfounded, Brian said, "What? Murdered?"

"Yeah. Everybody's been trying to call you. I went to the funeral. Lauren is holding up fine."

Brian sat down on the couch. "Oh man! I got to go check on her."

"You're probably the last person she wants to see."

Ignoring him, Brian got up to shower.

*   *   *

"Come in," Pat said with his eyes still on the magazine.

Manus walked in the cell and closed the door behind him. "What's up with you?"

Pat said, "Ain't shit."

"I thought you was going to meet me for breakfast this morning?"

Pat sat the magazine down and sighed. "I was, man, but then I was like fuck it."

Manus sat down in the chair. "You wasn't going to holla at me before I bounce?"

Pat flipped his palms up and then dropped them back to his lap.

Knowing what Pat was thinking, Manus scooted up in the chair. "Look, man. I'm not going to promise you that I'm going to write you everyday, but that's my word I'mma keep in touch. And as long as I'm straight, I'mma keep you straight."

"All of that *sounds* good."

"It's real. I know about the struggle in here, and I know how niggas be getting out and forgetting about the ones that held them down in here. I hate that shit, so there's no way I'm going to become what I hate. Feel me?"

"I feel you."

"I got you."

After a moment, Pat said, "I believe you."

Manus got up and Pat did the same. They gave each other dap and embraced. "So what are you going to do?"

"I'm not even going to front; I'mma get that bread. It's in my genes."

Pat nodded solemnly. He knew that a determined man's will was difficult if not impossible to change. "Just be careful." Then he said, "What about that Brad shit?"

"With something like that, I just got to play my cards right. I'mma stay low, keep my eyes and ears open, and I guarantee I'll get the scoop on it. And the sweet thing is don't nobody really know he's my man. We didn't hang on the streets. So I know a nigga is going to slip up, and that's when I'm going to do my thing."

Pat nodded. "That's exactly how I'd handle it."

"It's going down."

"All I can really say is stick to your grind and be careful."

"That's all I can do."

The men gave one another dap again.

Manus said, "Now come get these shoes and shit before I give them to Clark. He's been trying to cut-throat you all morning."

"I'll fuck around and cut *his* throat," Pat said as they walked out the cell.

*   *   *

Lauren's brother, Nelson, shook her lightly until she awoke. "What's wrong?" she asked.

"Somebody's at the door for you."

"Who is it?"

"Brian."

Lauren trembled with rage. "What in the hell does he want?"

Nelson put a hand on her shoulder. "Now, don't get all worked up. Just let him say what he has to say, and I'll send him about his way. Okay?"

Lauren reluctantly resigned. "I guess."

Nelson smiled. "Now remember, don't get worked up."

Lauren got herself together and went into the living room. She was shocked when she saw Brian. His once-well-managed afro was now mostly gray and thinning at the front.

Brian stood when she entered the room. "Lauren, I'm so sorry. I swear I just found out."

Lauren just nodded.

Then he said, "How did it happen? Do they know who done it?"

Lauren took a deep breath. It took everything she had not to rush him. Here, standing in front of her, was a man that had never shown any interest in anybody but himself. Now that Brad was gone, he was all of a sudden concerned. "All I know is he and some friends were shot after they left the club. As usual, ain't nobody seen nothing."

"What did Brad get himself into? Was he a gangbanger?"

Lauren ignored the comment. She didn't trust her temper right now.

"How are you holding up? Is there anything I can do for you?"

Lauren looked at him and wondered what he could possibly do to help her out. He looked like he was barely holding himself together. "Look, Brian. Why are you really here? I mean, you ain't never cared before. Why all of a sudden now?"

"How could you say that? I've always provided for Bradley."

"That was fucking child support! You had to pay that or go to jail!"

"Look, Lauren. I can see that this isn't going to work, so I'll just be frank with you. I'm in a jam right now. I'm broke. I know you had a big life insurance policy on Brad, and I think I'm entitled to at least half of that."

Lauren couldn't believe her ears. She screamed, "You low down dirty muthafucka!" She ran to the coffee table where crystal ornaments set. By the time she picked up a large crystal dish and threw it, Brian was running out the door.

CHAPTER 6

"May I speak to Ms. Lauren?"

"Hey, Manus! About time you called. I was starting to think that I had my dates mixed up."

"Nah, that bus just went all around the world before it got to Durham."

"Well, I'm happy that you're finally home. I know your mother will be, too."

"Uh, I know she will."

"So, what are you going to do now that you're out?"

"My uncle is going to give me a job at his cleaners."

"Stick with it, baby, because ain't nothing out there in those streets but trouble."

"I know, I know."

"Well, it's nice to hear from you."

"You too."

"What do you have planned for next Sunday?"

"Nothing."

"Would you like to come to dinner?"

"I would love to."

"You already have the address, so be here around four-thirty."

"Okay. Do you need me to bring anything?"

"No, baby. Just bring yourself. That alone is a blessing."

"I'll be there."

Manus ended the call and lay back on the *Lazy Boy*. He admired Lauren for being as strong as she was. Since Brad's death, she had set up a foundation in his name. The foundation helped victims' families cope with the loss of loved ones. It also provided financial assistance for families that didn't have life insurance or money to cover burial expenses. The foundation also now headed up the four-mile Stop the

Violence March that took place once a year.

Manus' uncle Grip walked into the living room and handed him some money.

"Here, go get yourself something to wear."

"Good look, Unc."

"You can take the Caddy."

"Word. Uh, Unc. I got to holla at you about something when I get back."

"A'ight."

Grip threw Manus the keys to his 2005 STS and Manus left.

After Manus had pulled off, Grip went to the liquor cabinet and poured himself a drink. He stared at a portrait on the wall.

"I'll keep my word, Leet. Don't worry. As long as I got it, he got it."

He stared at the portrait for a little while longer before walking out of the room.

Grip was a quiet and discrete man in his late forties. In his earlier years, he had been flamboyant and cocky until he'd lost his mentor. Along with that, he obtained custody of then twelve-year-old Manus. Grip knew he had to set an example, and longevity was vital.

In his twenty-three years of hustling, Grip had acquired a string of laundromats, two car lots, and a detail shop.

Raising Manus had been more challenging than anything in his life. Manus had been very curious and stubborn. Since the age of eighteen, Manus had been obsessed with getting in the drug game, but Grip forbade him. Grip didn't want him to take the route that he and Manus' father had taken.

But Manus, being the person he was, decided to do what he wanted to do. His plan was to build up enough money so that he could buy enough drugs to sell in quantities. Petty cash was beneath him. That very determination was what eventually sent him to prison for eight years.

*   *   *

The mall was different from how Manus remembered it. All the stores that he had once shopped at were now replaced with stores he'd never heard of. After carefully selecting his clothes, Manus stopped at Foot Locker for the finishing touches.

On his way out, someone called his name. He turned to see his ex, Erica. She walked up and gave him a hug. "Look at you, got muscles and all. How have you been?"

Manus didn't respond. He just observed her. Erica had gained thirty pounds since he had last seen her. The to-die-for body now had more rolls than curves. "I'm straight."

"How long have you been home?"

"Not long."

"I saw Grip one day and asked about you. He told me that you were coming home soon. He told you?"

"Nah."

"Why you talking like that? What, you don't want to talk to me?"

"You a'ight."

"Oh. You look good, though."

"Thank you. Well, I got to go. I'll holla." Manus turned to leave.

"Manus."

He turned around. "What's up?"

"Can I get your number so I can call you sometime?"

"Nah, that wouldn't be right."

"Why it wouldn't?"

"'Cause I ain't feeling that, that's why."

"You ain't feeling what?"

Manus took a deep breath before he spoke. "Look, Erica. I ain't trying to argue, but you wasn't thinking about a nigga when I was locked."

"Oh my God! I can't believe you're still tripping about that old-ass shit. Hell, I should be mad at you for involving me in that bullshit. What if you wouldn't have seen that police running behind you when you got in my car? They would've pulled me and took me to jail with your ass."

Manus laughed coldly and walked off. Erica was yelling something, but it was unintelligible to him.

*　　　*　　　*

As Manus drove home, he thought about the encounter that he just had with Erica. He was awed at the one-in-a-thousand odds of running into Erica on his first day out. The way she acted didn't surprise him. She had long since proven to him that she was pre-dictable.

When he returned home, Grip was in the den watching TV. Manus put his bags up and joined him.

Grip said, "Was that enough to get all you needed?"

"Yeah, that was enough. Thanks."

"I know how you like that hip hop stuff. If you youngins saved all the money you spent on that junk for a year, you would have enough to buy a house. Could rent it out or something." Grip paused, then said, "What's wrong with you?"

"Unc, guess who I just bumped into at the mall?"

"Who?"

"Erica."

"Yeah? I seen her about two months ago. She asked about you."

"She told me, with her crazy self."

"I never met one that wasn't in her own kind of way."

"Do you know she had the audacity to ask me for my number?"

"At my age, don't too much surprise me any more. See, it's like this with life: The sooner you lower your expectations of people the sooner you'll be happy — or more content with life." Grip let that sink in before continuing. "Now, what you had to talk to me about?"

Manus slid to the edge of his seat. "I 'preciate everything you ever done for me. I don't want to sound ungrateful or nothing, but I already know that the job at the cleaners ain't gonna work for me. I'm trying to come up."

Grip cocked his head. "What do you mean, *you're trying to come up*?"

"You know, the game. I got skills, and you can trust me."

Grip looked at him like he was some parasite on his couch. "Why are you so obsessed with that life?"

"I'm my father's son."

"So you think because your father was successful in that kind of life, you will be, too?"

Manus didn't respond.

Grip said, "I don't understand you. You got everything at your feet. You don't want for shit."

"No. You got everything at *your* feet. I don't got nothing. If it wasn't for you, I'll still be in those Chic jeans they sent me home in."

Grip just stared at him.

Manus said, "I know I haven't proven to you that I'm ready, but I am. That lil' stunt I pulled eight years ago was the dumbest thing I ever done. That wasn't me; that was something I did out of desperation."

Grip just continued to stare.

"Grip, you have held my hand too long. The ride is over. I got to stand up on my own." Manus started to leave.

"Sit down," Grip ordered.

Manus sat back down.

"I've always seen your father in everything you do, and it's scary. I love and respect that man. If it wasn't for him, I wouldn't be where I am today."

"You never told me that."

"Yep. He taught me everything I know."

"How come you never really talked to me about him before?"

"'Cause it was too painful. Still is."

Manus' mind began to pace. "So you're saying my Daddy taught you the game?"

"Everything I know."

"Then why won't you pass that knowledge to me? My Daddy gave you the same opportunity that I'm asking you for."

"What you're failing to realize is your father indulged for years in that treacherous game so he could open up avenues for you that he never had. He wasn't in the game so he could start up a family thing."

"I understand all of that. But you're failing to realize that this is what I want to do. This is what I'm going to do. Knowing that nothing can change my mind, why don't you just turn me on? I'm not a kid anymore."

"I can't."

"You can't? Why not?"

"'Cause me and your father made a promise that if anything ever happened to one of us, we would raise the other one's kids the right way."

"And you kept your promise. You making me a part of your team still doesn't change that. I swear, Grip, I wouldn't even be stressing this issue like this if I wasn't dead serious about it. I had a nice connect set up for me when I got out; Brad was gonna turn me on. But it died with him. Come on, Unc. I need this."

Grip was quiet for a moment; then he began to laugh.

Manus was baffled. "What's funny?"

"It's just that you remind me so much of your father. He was so determined to beat any obstacle in his way."

"That's right, Unc. With or without you, I'm gonna do this."

"Answer this for me. Are you aware of the consequences that come with the game?"

"Yeah."

"Do you know that a low percentage of people make it in the game without going in and out of jail?"

"Yeah."

Grip sighed. "Okay, I'll help you. But … there's one catch."

*　　　*　　　*

"Hello?" Shawnda answered.

Erica said, "Girl, guess who the fuck I seen at the mall today?"

"Who, bitch?"

"Manus."

"You lying!"

"No, I ain't, either. Girl, he was looking so good. Got muscles, done grew his hair and all."

"When he got out?"

"A few days ago, I guess."

"What was he talking about?"

"Nothing really. He's still mad at me for leaving him."

"That old-ass shit? He needs to get over that. It's a new day."

"That's what I told him."

"What he say about lil' Charles?"

"I ain't get the chance to tell him. He walked off too fast."

"Bitch, he gonna bug out when you tell him."

"I know."

"Well, I'll pick you up around nine."

"Okay, bye."

CHAPTER 7

Twenty-year-old Pedro Perez walked home from a long day of work at a local junkyard. He had just worked from six to six taking parts off of totaled cars to sell. The white guy that owned the junk yard paid Pedro and four other Mexicans seventy-five dollars a week under the table. Not a good salary for the year 1990.

Pedro lived with his mother and two younger sisters in a one-bedroom apartment. His mother worked as a housekeeper at a nearby hotel. Every day was a struggle for them.

As Pedro turned onto his street, he saw a crowd gathered in his yard, so he took off running to see what was going on. Once he reached the duplex, he saw that the commotion was on his neighbor's side. Pedro made his way inside and saw his neighbor Maria holding her twelve-year-old daughter. She was screaming obscenities at her husband.

"Look what they done to our daughter! And all you can do is cry? You coward!" Her husband sat down on the floor and put his head between his knees.

Pedro saw his mother sitting in the corner and went over to her. "What happened?"

"That black gang raped their daughter and took their money."

For the past month, a gang of young blacks had been invading homes in the Hispanic community. Not only had they robbed the Mexicans of their savings, they had also raped the wives and daughters.

Just as the Mexicans didn't trust the banks to hold their money, they didn't trust the police to handle their affairs. Plus, most of them were illegal immigrants. This was a widely known fact, and it made them high targets for crimes with minimal risk of being caught.

Pedro looked at the little girl, who was the same age as his younger sister, and felt sick to his stomach. He knew he had to put a stop to the gang. They had gotten too close for his comfort. He headed home, which was right next door.

In his apartment, Pedro bent down at the hot water heater that sat inside an aluminum frame. He popped off the panel on the side and stuck his hand in. He felt around until he located the long barrel .38.

*   *   *

The TIC crew of four sat under the pavilion in the park. It was dark and raining heavily. The men's ages ranged from fourteen to twenty. Dee, who was twenty years old and the leader, took a long drag on a joint that was laced with crack and marijuana. He passed it to T.J., who was fourteen, then took a swig from his 40 ounce.

"From now on we gonna hit them amigos up three times a week."

T.J. said, "Can we rape them every time, too?"

Dee frowned and looked over to his cousin, Mike. "You better tell that nigga what our name is."

Mike looked at T.J. "Nigga, we're the Take It Clique. Whatever we want we gonna take it."

Max, the quiet one, drained his 40 ounce and twisted another one open. He said to Dee, "Since we done got away with a few jux, you want to start doing more? Them amigos ain't gonna keep letting us do that shit to them."

"Man, them wetbacks ain't gonna put five-o on us. Them mutha-fuckas don't even got no green card, so they ain't trying to draw no heat on themselves. If you scared, just say you scared. But don't try to dissuade us."

"I ain't scared of shit. And I ain't talking about them putting the police on us."

"Then what the fuck you talking about then?"

"Them amigos is just like us. They ruff necks."

"Ain't no goddamn Mexican like me! My uncle told me that if you ain't black, then you white. And best believe them amigos are more white than black."

"You better quit listening to your crazy-ass uncle and all of that

Five Percenter bullshit, 'cause Mexicans are like us."

T.J., who was too naive to detect the tension in the air, said, "Ahh!"

Dee stared at Mike and stood. He approached him. "For one, let my uncle's name taste like shit in your mouth. For two, I'm the goddamn leader of TIC, and if I say that we gonna rob every day, then that's what the fuck we gonna do."

As soon as Max sat his beer down to stand up, Mike stood and walked to Dee's side. Max stayed seated.

Dee said, "I've noticed how you always be challenging my wisdom and shit like you want my position or something."

"Nigga, I don't want your muthafucking position. Fuck —"

Mike smashed Max across the head with the 40 ounce bottle.

Max fell to the floor, and the men started kicking him in the face and ribs. When the two men tired themselves out, Dee pulled Max's head up by his high-top fade. "Listen, you muthafucking Mexican lover; you better watch your goddamn mouth when you're talking to me! Something ain't right about your ass anyway. I've noticed how every time we get us some Mexican pussy, you don't never get you none."

Mike said, "Yeah, nigga. Either you a Mexican lover or you're gay."

"Matter of fact, it don't even matter. Get your Mexican, man-loving ass away from here. We don't fuck with you no more." Dee and Mike grabbed the man by his arms and threw him out of the pavilion.

Max struggled to his feet and walked away holding his ribs. As he walked through the rain, he stopped under a tree and vomited. That's when he heard the gunshots.

*   *   *

Dee lit another laced joint and looked at T.J. "Why you all quiet now?"

T.J. shrugged. "I was just thinking, that's all."

"Well, I hope it ain't about that faggot-ass nigga. 'Cause if it is, then you can get the same treatment."

"Uh, nah. I ... I'm just ready to run up in another house. Yeah."

Mike and Dee started laughing. "That's what I'm talking about. You like that young pussy, don't you?"

"Hell yeah. It was good."

The men began to laugh again, but it was cut short by gunfire. Before they knew what was happening, bullets were ripping through their bodies. Dee, who took a bullet to the head, laid face-down, dead. Mike laid semi-conscious beside him, with two bullets in his side. T.J., who was conscious with a bullet in his chest, lay paralyzed with fear. He saw a man squat at each of his friends and do something.

Finally the gunman walked over and started unfastening T.J.'s pants. He saw that the boy was still alive and said in Spanish, "I won't give you the chance to rape my sisters."

After Max watched the Mexican disappear in some nearby woods, he came out of his hiding spot and ran over to the men. He bent down to reach inside Dee's pockets. When he saw the severed penis lying beside Dee, Max scrambled away and vomited again.

*   *   *

The next day, news of the brutal murders spread through the city like wildfire. Fearing the Mexicans wouldn't stop until he, too, was dead, Max bought a one-way bus ticket and went to live with his aunt in Cleveland.

The Hispanic community praised Pedro and threw a fiesta for him. From that day forward, Pedro would be the most respected man in the community. Any problems, they would call on Pedro to handle things. They decided to give him a more fitting name. He was Amado, which means "beloved" in Spanish.

A rising drug dealer soon heard about Amado and eventually met and offered him three hundred dollars a week to be his enforcer/body guard. Amado accepted it.

CHAPTER 8

Amado pulled up at the private-owned shooting range in his new Ford Expedition. He got out and walked over to where his boss stood. Amado was tall for a Mexican. He was six feet three and weighed two hundred pounds. Acne craters covered his face, so he kept a full beard. Most of the clothing he owned was black.

Jose saw him and shook his hand. "Amado." Then he gestured to a man at his right side. "You already met my cousin Gonzales."

Amado shook the young man's hand. "How are you doing?"

"Fine, and you?"

"I'm fine."

Then Jose said to his cousin, "Can you excuse us for a moment?"

"Sure." He walked off.

Jose said, "He's going to be working with you from now on."

"Why? You think I need help now?"

"No, of course not. I'm hiring him so you can have more time with your family."

"I don't need more time off. My family understands my duties."

"Amado, how long have you worked for me?"

"Fifteen years."

"And how many times have you ever taken off?"

"None."

"That's what I mean. You need to take some time off."

"You going to trust an inexperienced guy to watch over things? He can't be no older than twenty, twenty-one."

"He's the same age you were when you started. Plus, he's a marksman. Been shooting since he was ten."

"But that don't have anything to do with seeing situations before they happen."

"You're right. But still, I'm not going to do anything major on your days off. At the most, go shopping or out to eat. So relax. Take a few days off."

Reluctantly, Amado agreed.

*   *   *

Manus looked over at Grip, who was driving. "Unc, when did you get out the game?"

"About a year after you got locked up."

"Why? That was your livelihood."

"The way the feds were scooping up my associates, I realized my businesses were generating enough money for me. I know when to say when. Them feds scare the hell out of me."

After a moment, Manus said, "Do the Elks Lodge be rocking like that?"

"Yeah, that's where the real happenings is at. I wish Mercy Dee's was still open. Now that's a real club."

"My dad used to go there; I remember."

"Yeah, he loved that club. He even tried to buy it."

"What, the owner didn't want to sell it?"

"He would have been a fool to, as many people that came there every week."

Manus' mood changed. "Why she had to kill him?"

After a moment Grip said, "I guess she done it because she was hurt. But I know for a fact that she regrets it to this day."

"Why, 'cause she's locked up?"

"No, 'cause she knows how much it affected you."

Manus was silent.

"When are you going to see her?"

"Who?" Manus asked, knowing.

"Your mother."

"Soon," he lied.

"I talked to her about a week ago, but I didn't tell her that you were about to get out. I wanted you to surprise her."

"To be honest with you, I really don't have nothing to say to her."

"That's your mother. There's plenty to say. You can start by confronting your differences with her."

"It's not going to bring my daddy back."

"No, it won't. But, still, you have a mother left. Some people would give anything just to have that."

Manus didn't respond. Every time he thought about his father, his resentment grew for his mother. He loved his mother, but her efforts were always overshadowed by his father's big efforts.

Big Leet was a generous and understanding man. Growing up poor with no father, he'd made a promise to himself that if he ever had kids, he would give them the world. So, in the twelve years that he was in Manus' life, he had done just that. When he was murdered, life didn't seem all that important to Manus anymore. And ever since, he had refused to speak to his mother. She had taken his best friend away from him, and for that he could never forgive her.

*   *   *

When he and Manus entered the club, Grip was greeted by several people before reaching the bar.

Manus said, "I see you the man up in here."

"Nah, they're just friendly, that's all. What you drinking?"

"No, Unc. Let me buy you something for a change."

"I don't have a problem with that. Get me a double shot of Easy Jesus."

"Easy Jesus?"

"Yeah. E & J."

"Oh. I like that Paul better."

"Yeah, that's smooth. But I've been on Easy Jesus forever; don't nothing else taste right."

"Did my dad drink?"

"A lil' bit."

"What did he drink?"

Grip cleared his throat and said, "Paul."

*   *   *

"Momma," Lil' Charles whined. "You about to go to the club again?"

Erica said, "You know where I go every Friday. Don't ask me no dumb shit like that. Where's your sister at?"

"In the living room with daddy."

"Don't you think that's where you need to be?"

"Yeah, but I came to ask is you gonna cook before you leave?"

"Hell nah. Ain't your daddy in there?"

"Yeah, but he don't be cooking right."

"Well, your ass better eat some cereal then."

Lil' Charles walked away stomping his feet and mumbling.

Erica screamed, "You better quit all that goddamn stomping before I give your ass something to stomp for!" Then she said to herself, "Crazy-ass kids. Get on my goddamn nerves!"

Charles Sr. yelled, "Erica, somebody's out there blowing."

Erica grabbed her things and ran to the door. Kandis, who was only four, jumped off the couch and ran up to her mother. "Momma, give me a kiss before you leave."

"Girl, I ain't about to mess up my makeup fucking with you. Then she turned to Charles Sr. "Charles, fix them something to eat."

After she left, Charles Sr. looked at Kandis and said, "What do you want daddy to cook you, baby?"

Kandis frowned. "I just want some cereal."

*   *   *

Erica got in the car and said to Shawnda, "Hey, girl."

Observing her, Shawnda said, "What's up, bitch? That dress ain't never fit me like that. I guess my stomach was too big or something."

"Girl, mine is, too. That shit won't go down for nothing."

"What are you doing to bring it down?"

"A lot of fucking."

"Me too, bitch." The women laughed.

"You think it's the shot that's blowing us up? Shawnda asked.

"I don't know … it might be."

"It might not be, though. Look at Keyona. She's on the shot and she's skinny as hell."

"Yeah, but you know they say she got that shit. Fucking with Black."

"I heard."

"All these niggas are fucked up."

"I know. All the good ones are already taken. Or locked up."

"That's why I need to work at a prison. Find me a nigga with some money and blow his mind. Especially one that's been locked up for a while. Some head would make him tell me where the stash is at." The women started laughing and gave one another high-fives.

Erica and Shawnda had been best friends since the eighth grade. Shawnda was a brown-skinned, stout woman with a high forehead. She was only five foot three, but had the booming voice of a giant. Next to having multiple sex partners, her favorite thing to do was gossip about who, what, when, and where. And if it was a really hot topic, she would call Erica no matter what time it was.

"Have you told Charles about Lil' Charles yet?" Shawnda asked.

"Not yet. First I want to see if Manus gonna step up to the plate. If he don't then I still got Charles. You feel me?"

"Hell nah, bitch! You crazy as hell. Didn't you say Manus still fucks with his uncle?"

"Uh huh."

"And do you know how much money Grip got?"

"Not really, but I know he owns a detail shop or something."

"Bitch, he owns more than that. He's a kingpin. If you ask me, I think he runs the city on the low."

"I do remember Manus saying something about his uncle like that, but I had forgot."

"I know everything about him. I've been trying to get that nigga for the longest. And I'm gonna get him if that's the last thing I do. And if you know like I know, bitch, you better get that bread out of Manus. And if possible, get him back. He's bound to blow."

Erica thought about that for a moment and said, "I think he hates me, though."

"Bitch, you're his baby's momma! All men hate their baby's momma but know they got the best pussy. It'll be nothing to get him back once he finds out he got a son by you. Watch."

After a moment, Erica said, "So what's up with Dread? He still tripping about the money you stole from him?"

"He was … until I told him I was pregnant."

"Girl, you can't get pregnant. You're on the shot."

"Okay. We know that, but he don't."

"So what are you going to do when you ain't showing in four months?"

"You already know. Tell him I had a miscarriage."

CHAPTER 9

Grip drained his fifth glass of brandy and said, "Have you got a shot of pussy since you been home?"

"Nah. I could've, but I ain't stressed. I went eight years without it."

"Pick any woman in here and I'll make it happen."

"Come on, Unc. I don't need no help in that department. My game is tight. I'm just on a paper chase right now."

"Be patient. It'll come. I guarantee that."

Just then, a brown-skinned man with a shaved head and a goatee approached them. His walk was the slow, deliberate swagger of a pimp.

Grip smiled when he saw the man. "Six, my main man. What's happening?"

The men shook hands, and in a muffled voice Six said, "Ain't nothing, partner. Just taking it one day at a time."

Grip leaned back and took in Six's attire. "If dressing sharp was a crime, you would've been caught a life sentence back in the seventies."

Six had on white slacks, a white dress shirt with light blue pinstripes in it, and some white and light blue gator shoes. "I'm just trying to keep up with you, that's all."

"This is my nephew, Manus." Then he turned to Manus. "This is one of my oldest friends, Six."

Six clamped Manus' hand in both of his. "It's a pleasure to meet you."

"Same here," Manus said, wondering why Six still held his hand.

"There's something vaguely familiar about this young man. Tell me this isn't whose son I think it is."

Grip said, "It is. This is who I wanted you to meet."

Suddenly Six's smile was gone and there was a seriousness about him. "I owe so much to your father. He was a great man. If you ever need anything, please don't hesitate to ask."

Grip stole a glance at Manus.

Six produced a card and gave it to Manus.

Grip said, "He's trying to get his feet wet."

Reading between the lines, Six took the toothpick out of his mouth and said to Manus, "You sure? It's cold out there."

"I'll adapt."

"With your bloodline, I know you will. Call me in the morning."

The men talked until a woman walked up and took Six to the dance floor. Grip said, "That's a good man right there. I trust him with my life."

"How he know Big Leet?"

"Leet saved his life."

"Yeah? How?"

"About twenty years ago, Six got into an altercation with this dude and it resulted in gunplay. Six's gun jammed and he got hit. When the dude was about to finish him, Leet intervened and tried to reason with him … but the dude was hot-headed. So in the end, Leet ended up killing the guy."

"So my daddy did some time, too?"

"Not Leet. He didn't even know what the inside of a police car looked like."

"He must've been real careful."

"He was. Plus, people minded their business back then. To be a snitch then meant that you were the scum at the bottom of the barrel. But now, that shit is like a sport."

"All-star teams and stuff."

Grip nodded sadly. "But even in death, Leet can't escape Six. He visits Leet's grave site on every birthday and death anniversary."

*   *   *

"Bitch, let him finger you. He'll let you in for free."

Erica said, "That ain't gonna work for me."

"Why it ain't?"

"'Cause I'm on my period."

The women walked up to the doorman, and he smiled when he saw Shawnda. "What's up, Shawnda?"

"Hey, Block. What's up with you?"

"You." Block stared down at Shawnda's cleavage. "You're looking scrumptious as usual."

Shawnda came closer to him and whispered, "Look, I'm getting bored with all this foreplay. I'm trying to see what you're working with."

"*Sheeit*, you can see tonight."

"Well, I guess I will then. I'll be waiting at your car, but I got to take my girlfriend home first."

"That's cool."

Shawnda grabbed Erica's arm and eased past Block.

After they were inside the club Erica said, "Girl, you terrible."

"Fuck it, bitch. They use us all the time."

"You gonna give him some for real?"

"I might let him pay for some. That's if I don't find a higher bidder meanwhile."

"Girl, I'm about to get drunk while they still letting women drink free."

"Oh my God!" Shawnda said, stopping in her tracks. "Look who's at the bar."

When Erica saw Manus, she began patting her hair. "How I look, Girl?"

"Like a top-notch gold digger. Go get him, bitch."

Erica took off and Shawnda trailed.

When they reached the men, Manus stared at Erica blankly.

"What's up, Manus?"

He nodded.

"What's up, Grip? How are you doing?"

"I'm doing good."

Then Shawnda stepped up. "What's up, Grip? Remember me?"

"Yeah, I remember you."

Erica said to Manus, "Can I talk to you for a minute? It's important."

Irritated, Manus said, "About what?"

"It's private."

Manus sighed and said, "Unc, I'll be right back."

Shawnda looped her arm with Grip's and said, "I got him; he ain't going nowhere."

Manus walked off.

Shawnda said, "So, what are you getting into tonight?"

Grip casually pulled his arm from hers and said, "My bed."

"Can I come, too?"

"You won't give up, huh?"

She licked her lips. "When I'm hungry for something, I don't stop until I get it."

*   *   *

"What is it?" Manus asked.

"Remember when you first got locked and I told you that I got an abortion?"

"Uh huh."

"Well, I didn't."

"And?"

"And I had your son."

Manus laughed. "Whatever."

"Come on, Manus. You know I wouldn't play about nothing like that."

"I don't know shit. Especially nothing about you."

"That's on my life."

"I know you don't expect me to go for that after all this time."

"All you got to do is see him. He looks exactly like you."

"What the fuck are you trying to pull?"

"I ain't trying to pull shit. I'm just letting you know about your son."

"Well, there's only one thing to do then."

"And what's that?"

"Get a blood test."

"You gonna pay for it, right?"

"I know *you* ain't."

"You ain't got to act like that. At least I was woman enough to tell you."

Manus laughed coldly. "What the fuck ever. Just give me your number so I can let you know when the appointment is."

Erica got a pen from the bar and wrote a number down on a

napkin. "This is Shawnda's number. Just leave the —"

"I ain't trying to talk to that broad."

"Well, I don't know how you gonna get in touch with me then. 'Cause I don't got a phone."

Manus accepted the number and walked back over to Grip. He noticed that Shawnda was watching him intently. "What is it?" he snapped.

Shawnda rolled her eyes and said to Grip, "So, you gonna let me know before you leave, right?"

"Yeah, I'll let you know."

As soon as she left, Manus said, "You ain't gonna believe what that broad told me."

"What's that?"

"That she got a son by me."

"What? How in the hell can you have a son by her?"

"I know she was supposedly pregnant when I first got locked up, but she told me she got an abortion."

"Well, you know what you got to do then, right?"

"Get a blood test."

"Damn right. I'll loan you the money." He smiled then walked away, headed toward a table of women.

Thirty minutes later, Grip appeared at Manus' side and handed him the keys to the Range Rover. "Look, I'll catch up with you in the morning. My friend don't want to sleep alone tonight." Manus looked at a stunning woman as she stood behind Grip.

"Damn, Unc. She's a dime."

"She's a'ight. More spoiled than anything."

"Shawnda gonna get you," Manus said, laughing.

"Man, I ain't thinking about that stalker. She knows every one of my cars. Scares me a little."

"And you should be."

"Well, let me go. Be careful."

"I will."

Grip put his arm around the waist of the lady and exited the building. Manus noticed Shawnda and Erica looking at the lady with grim expressions on their faces.

*   *   *

In the Range Rover, Manus listened to Frankie Beverly and Maze's *Joy and Pain*. It was the story of his life. Although he was disturbed by Erica's news, he pushed it away by focusing on the good news concerning Six. He knew that nothing could stop him now. He decided to celebrate by treating himself at his favorite restaurant.

Upon entering Honey's, he was immediately seated.

One of the most beautiful dark-skinned women that he ever saw walked up and handed him a menu. With a foreign accent she said, "How are you?"

Manus was tongue-tied.

"You okay?" she asked.

"Yeah, yeah. I'm tripping."

Confused, she said, "Tripping?"

Manus realized that she didn't understand the slang, and said, "I'm just tired."

"Oh, sleepy. Want some coffee?"

"Yes, that's exactly what I need."

"Okay, I'll get that for you. Are you ready to order, or do you need some time?"

"No, I'm ready to order, Ge —," he said, struggling to pronounce the name on her nametag.

"It's pronounced Ba-Lou, but my friends call me Gee."

"A beautiful name for a beautiful face."

Gee smiled. "Thank you."

*   *   *

For the next four days, Manus visited Honey's four times before building up the nerve to ask Gee for her number. He wasn't the shy type; he was just intimidated by her beauty.

Gee was an Egyptian who had been in the states for four years. She was finishing her last semester in dentistry at the University of North Carolina. Although they did not have much in common, a magnetic force seemed to pull them together.

Six had finally familiarized Manus with his operation. Manus was a fast learner, a natural. In one area, Manus was so gifted that Six decided to make it his sole job. Manus had mastered the art of cooking cocaine. He could cook and shape it in many different ways. His job was to cook for Six's main customers at a set price per kilo. Each customer would bring no less than five kilos.

*   *   *

Manus rang the doorbell and waited. Fifteen seconds later, a woman opened the door wearing a pink Roc-a-Wear velour suit. He smiled and said, "I'm Manus."

"Manus!"

"Hey, Ms. Lauren," he said, embracing her.

"Come on in, baby." She led him through the immaculate living room that was full of crystal and African art. When they reached the den Lauren said, "Have a seat; make yourself comfortable."

Manus sat down. "You have a nice house."

"Thank you. It took me three years to decorate it."

"Three years well spent."

"Thank you. So, how's your job going?"

"Well, actually I haven't started yet."

"Oh, I see."

Lauren stood. "Let me go check on this food. I hope you like seafood."

"The last time I checked, I did. The only seafood I had in the last eight years was the square fish that the prison served."

"No, baby. This isn't square fish." Lauren walked out of the den.

Manus observed the pictures on the wall. One picture caused him to get out of his seat to get a closer look. The picture was of Brad at around fifteen years old. He was standing beside a dirt bike, smiling.

"He begged me for two years to buy him that bike," Lauren said as she walked up beside Manus. "I was so scared that he was going to kill himself on it that I bought two sets of protection gear."

Manus could hear the grief in her voice. He blinked back tears.

Then she said, "I did all I could do to raise him right, but a mother can only do so much. It broke my heart when I found out that he was selling drugs. I could never go to sleep until I heard him come in. I hate to say this, but I got a lot of sleep when he went to prison. I didn't have to worry about getting that call in the middle of the night saying my son was dead." She hesitated. "And you know what? I still ended up getting that call. He was all I had. I dedicated my whole life to him by doing everything that I could. But ... but I guess I didn't ..." Lauren broke down crying and Manus embraced her.

"Don't blame yourself. You did all you could."

"When I give those speeches for Brad's foundation," Lauren sobbed, "I tell those mothers that they have to be strong and allow their deceased loved ones to live on through them. But ... I can't do it no more. It just hurts too much to keep thinking and talking about him, knowing that he's never coming back. I'm going crazy."

Lauren's knees buckled, but Manus caught her and took her to the couch. He could smell a faint scent of alcohol on her breath. Lauren put her head on his shoulders and shook violently.

"It's going to be a'ight. Please stop crying."

"But how can it? Brad's not coming back. I don't have nobody."

Manus twisted his body toward her and put his hands on her shoulders. With his eyes locked to hers he said, "You have me. And I promise that I'm not going anywhere."

Lauren leaned forward and kissed Manus on his lips.

The kiss felt wrong, so Manus pulled back.

Lauren put her hands to her mouth. "Oh my God! I'm sorry, Manus."

She got up to leave the room, but Manus grabbed her arm and hugged her. "It's okay, Ms. Lauren."

"I just feel so alone right now. The police act like they could care less about who killed Brad. The investigating officer didn't even know who Brad was when I called him for an update on the case. Brad's soul won't be able to rest until the person that killed him faces justice. And neither will mine."

"Don't worry, Ms. Lauren. Whoever killed him gonna get theirs. I promise."

Chapter 10

Kim sat on her car and watched as two men loaded furniture on a truck. When Lauren pulled next door, Kim decided to walk over there.

"Hey, Lauren."

Lauren glanced at the men loading the Ryder truck then turned back to Kim. "What's going on? I know you're not moving on me."

Kim dropped her head and nodded.

"But why?"

"Before I met Br ... your son, I was playing with the idea already. But he showed up and I fell in love. I love you, Lauren, but I'll never be able to get over him if I'm around you everyday."

Lauren simply nodded.

Kim grabbed her hand. "Please don't be mad at me."

Lauren hugged her. "I'm not. I just want you to come see me from time to time."

"I'll try to on holidays."

"You're talking like you're moving to the other side of the world."

"Almost. I'm moving to Seattle to live with my cousin."

"Oh."

"I left my address and phone number on your answering machine."

Tears began to run down Lauren's face, and she embraced Kim again. "I've gotten so attached to you. I swear I wish you would stay."

"I wish, but I have so many bad memories here that seem to outweigh the good ones. I feel like this is my only chance to redeem my sanity."

Lauren sighed. "I understand. I want you to do whatever you have to do to get yourself together. Find your peace, baby. It's priceless."

*　　　*　　　*

Meat turned his head sideways to see if his hair covered the scar on his head. Once he was satisfied, he licked his lips and left from in front of the mirror. "Are you ready?" he asked the six-foot blonde sitting on the couch.

"Gosh, Meat," Wendy said, tapping the blunt's ashes in the ashtray. "You take longer to get ready than I do."

"I told you don't come over here 'til six."

"I came early because I know you. You only give me two hours of your time."

"So you decided to come early to get some more time in, huh?"

"I got to beat your system somehow."

"You're getting too slick for me."

"I got slick from being around you."

Meat smiled. He liked Wendy. She wasn't the average dingy blonde that he had been with. She was funny, sexy and, most of all, she showered him with gifts.

"Oh," she said. "Some girl called your phone while you were in the shower."

"You answered my phone?"

"I wasn't, but it just kept ringing. I thought it might have been an emergency, so I answered it."

"Who was it?"

"Some girl named Tasha. She wouldn't talk to me like she had some sense, so I hung up on her."

Oh shit! Meat thought. Then he said, "How long ago was this?"

"Like ten minutes ago."

"You ready?"

"You don't want to finish smoking the blunt?"

"I'll smoke it in the car."

"I thought you didn't like smoking and riding?"

"I don't, but I don't have anything on me."

"Okay. I'm ready then."

Meat grabbed his keys and they headed out the door. As soon as they got in the car, a dark blue Mazda 626 pulled in behind them and blocked them in.

"Oh shit," Meat said softly.

Wendy turned around in her seat. "Who is that?"

"The woman you hung up on."

Wendy saw Tasha get out of the car and said, "That little bitch. I'm going to beat her ass if she says anything to me that I don't like."

Tasha walked to the driver's side of the CLK Mercedes and opened the door. "Bitch, what was all that shit you was talking on the phone?"

"Who are you calling a bitch?" Wendy asked as she attempted to get out of the car.

"No, you don't, bitch!" Tasha said as she started landing blows against Wendy's face and head. Wendy tried to defend herself but the position she was in made it impossible for her. After too many well-placed punches, all the fight was gone out of Wendy, and she began to scream for Meat.

"He can't help you, bitch!"

Tasha grabbed Wendy by the hair and dragged her out of the car and to the ground.

Once Tasha began to stomp Wendy, Meat knew he had to break it up. He got out and grabbed Tasha in a bear hug. "Okay, okay. You got off."

As Meat pulled her to his front door, Tasha spat at Wendy, "Don't you ever come out your mouth fucked up again!"

Once Meat took Tasha in his house, he came back outside and helped Wendy up. Her whole face was red.

"You okay?"

"I'm … I'm going to call the police on her."

"Don't bring that heat to my house, Wendy. You'll have *me* mad if you do."

"But she —"

"Still," he said, cutting her off, "that don't got shit to do with me. You want me to go to jail?"

"If you do, you know I'll get you out."

"Wendy, what do I care about that when I ain't trying to go at all?"

"I see what you're saying. I'm not going to call them."

"I'll call you later, okay? Go clean yourself up."

"Okay. Tell that bit —" She looked at the house door and saw that it was still closed. "Tell that bitch to let me out."

* * *

"Where you say y'all were going?" Charles Sr. asked Erica.

"I'm taking Lil' Charles to the hospital."

"What's wrong with him? He don't look sick to me."

"Oh, nah, I'm just taking him for a checkup."

"Well, why you can't take Kandis with you?"

"'Cause I asked you to watch her, that's why."

"When am I gonna get a break?"

"When she turns eighteen." Erica grabbed Lil' Charles's arm and left.

On the way to the Human Resource Center, Erica knew her life was about to change dramatically. She didn't know how, but she just knew that it would. She had nothing to lose by allowing a blood test to be conducted.

When they reached the center, Erica saw that Manus was already there. He didn't acknowledge her, he only stared at Lil' Charles.

Lil' Charles said, "Ma, who that man looking at me?"

"That's your real daddy."

"But I thought Daddy was my real daddy."

"Well, he ain't."

In a cubicle station, a pudgy black nurse swabbed the mouths of Manus and Charles.

"How accurate are these tests? Manus asked.

"They're 99.8% accurate." After she put the swabs in separate bags, the nurse said, "Okay, that's it. Come back in four hours and I'll have the results."

Manus pulled her aside and whispered, "Miss, is there any way I can get those results back sooner?"

"Four hours is extremely fast. Most places usually take forty-eight hours."

"I know, I know. But, Miss, it's vital that I get those results sooner. Would a tip speed things up?"

The nurse licked her lips. "Give me three hundred and I'll be able to tell you in an hour. I'll have to persuade the technician to put the other work aside for you."

Manus pulled out his wallet and gave her the money. "An hour."

*   *   *

José gave the kilo to the man and said in Spanish, "This is all I have until Friday."

The man grabbed the brick. "I need more. This will not last ten minutes. There's no cocaine on my side of town."

"Like I said, this is the best that I can do until Friday."

"Please, José. If you can get some more sooner, I'll buy double of what I usually get."

"Double?"

"Yes. I really need some more, but you are the only one that I trust to buy from."

Shaking his head, José said, "I can't even if I wanted to. I can't move without Amado."

Gonzalez, who was sitting in the corner observing the men, stood up when he heard the comment. "Excuse me," he said to the customer. Then he said to José, "Let me talk to you for a moment."

The men stepped to the other side of the room.

"What is it, Gonzalez?"

"I overheard you say that you couldn't make any moves without Amado present."

"Yeah, that's right."

"But that's what you got me for."

"But —"

"Come on, José. Let me show you that I'm qualified. If I mess up in any kind of way, fire me. And I promise I'll never bother you again."

José gave it some thought and realized that the task of getting some more coke wasn't a risky one. He had been dealing with Six for years without incidents. He knew that Amado would be disappointed when he found out, but José didn't care. After all, he was the boss. José said, "Okay, I'm going to test you out."

*   *   *

Manus sat in Fuddruckers and wondered how he had let Erica talk him into taking them to lunch. Erica sat silently with a smirk on her face that aggravated him. When the waitress brought their food, Manus took the bun off of his burger and added fries. He looked up and dropped his bun when he saw that Lil' Charles was doing the same thing.

Erica noticed Manus' burger and said, "So that's where he gets that shit from. It irks the fuck out of me."

Manus ignored her and said to Lil' Charles, "What grade are you in, lil' man?"

"Second grade."

"When is your birthday?"

"February the twenty-sixth."

Manus quickly calculated the months and saw that it was a possibility. The more he looked at the boy the more that he saw familiarities in him. Manus silently prayed that those features were coincidental. He couldn't imagine having to deal with Erica for the years to come.

Lil' Charles looked at Manus and said, "So you're my real daddy for real?"

"I don't know yet, but we'll know when we get back to the center."

"If you is, is my other daddy gonna be mad?"

Manus looked at Erica, and Lil' Charles followed suit.

"He might, but don't you want to know who your real daddy is?"

"Yeah, I guess." Then he looked back at Manus. "How come I ain't never seen you before? Where you been?"

"None of your business!" Erica spat.

Manus said, "He's a'ight. Chill." Then he said, "You haven't seen me before because I was somewhere where people go for being bad."

"Jail?"

"Yep."

"What, my momma didn't want to bring me to come see you?"

"I guess not."

*   *   *

Back at the center, Manus took a deep breath and walked in. As soon as he saw the nurse, he knew what the answer was.

She smiled and extended her hand. "Congratulations, Mr. Parrish. You're the father."

*   *   *

Six sat in his richly decorated den and waited for his wife Genie to escort his guest in.

L walked in and said, "Six, what's up with you?"

"Ain't nothing, partner. What's going on with you? You a'ight?"

"Yeah, I'm good. It's the world that's all wrong."

"I hear that. Have a seat." Then Six said, "My amigos are coming in town today. They wasn't supposed to come until Friday, but I guess they changed their minds. I got some things to take care of here, so I need you to handle that for me."

"Word."

"You can knock off two G's of what you owe me for doing it. Is that straight?"

"That's gravy."

"These are some of my main customers, so treat them with respect."

"All the time."

Six gave him the rest of the details and they loaded the coke in the car.

CHAPTER 11

T wo hours later, L pulled into the car wash with Tee and studied the scene. To his left he saw a green Suburban parked beside the vacuum. To his right a man was washing an older model Thunderbird. The carwash was the ideal place for privacy. It sat in an isolated area on a back street.

When L got out of the car, two Mexicans got out of the Suburban and walked up to him.

"What's up, amigo?" L said, as he shook their hands.

The Mexican with the crew cut said, "Nothing much, holmes. Are you Six's people?"

"Yeah. He couldn't make it, but it's good, though. You José?"

"Yeah."

"What's his name?" L asked, gesturing at the Mexican with the ponytail.

"That doesn't matter, holmes. Who's your friend?"

"That's my man. He's cool."

"Six didn't say nothing about two people."

"I know you ain't think I was coming here alone, did you? It's too much bread involved. Somebody might get tempted."

"José reached under his shirt. "You accusing me of trying to rip you off, holmes?"

Ponytail reached under his shirt also.

L threw his hands in the air. "No, amigo. I ain't mean it like that. I'm just saying."

José relaxed some and brought his hand from under his shirt. Then he nodded at Ponytail, who did the same. "Okay, holmes. Let's just do business and get it over with."

L put his hands down and motioned for Tee to get out.

Tee got out and popped the trunk.

The men gathered around to see. Ponytail opened one of the two gym bags and picked up one of the packages. After opening and tasting it, he nodded affirmatively at José.

José said to L, "I hope the other bag contains the same thing."

"Most definitely."

José looked at Ponytail. "Vete a recoger la plata."

Ponytail nodded and walked back to the Suburban. When he returned with a bag of his own, he handed it to L then reached for the cocaine in the trunk.

The guy washing the Thunderbird dropped the sud brush and rushed the men with a semi-automatic handgun. "Don't nobody move! Y'all know what it is."

The men were caught off guard. They froze in place as the armed man snatched the bag of money out of L's hand. He then checked each man, finding guns on the Mexicans.

José turned to Ponytail. "Nos tendieron una trampa." Then he turned to L. "You have made a big mistake, holmes."

* * *

Gonzales lay in the back of the Suburban with a Tech-9 in his hand. He watched as the deal went down through a special mirror that hung from the ceiling of the SUV. In a way, he had been praying for something to go wrong so that he could prove to José that he was just as good as Amado.

When he saw the armed man rush his friends, Gonzales squealed in delight. He kissed the rosary around his neck and eased out of the SUV.

* * *

L said, "What the fuck are you talking about? This ain't none of my doing. For all I know, you set this shit up. Six ain't gonna let this shit ride."

"Shut the fuck up!" The gunman screamed, "Before I set your ass on fire. Now grab them bags and walk with me. And the rest of ya'll better not move."

When L grabbed the bags from the trunk, he caught a glimpse

of a third Mexican crouching down on the side of the Suburban.

When Gonzales noticed that L had spotted him, he put an index finger to his lips.

L casually reached under his shirt and pulled out a black handgun.

Before Gonzales knew what was happening, three slugs were tearing at his neck and face.

The shots startled Rome, the initial robber, causing him to shoot Ponytail in the heart.

L screamed, "Goddamn, Rome! You suppose to know how many of them were in the truck!"

"He must've been laying down somewhere or something, 'cause I ain't see him."

Tee, who now had his gun out and trained on José, said, "What about this one?"

L said, "The plan is fucked up now. Put your work in and let's get the fuck out of here."

Tee looked at José and grinned.

José said, "You black bastard." Then he spat in Tee's face.

Not bothering to wipe, Tee squeezed ten shots into José's body before it hit the ground.

*   *   *

When L walked into Six's living room, Six was on the phone and motioned for him to sit. Then he said into the phone, "Well, let me call you back … A'ight then, bye." Six hung up and said, "You took care of that for me?"

L shook his head. "Hell nah. The po-po had the whole spot on lock."

"What happened?"

"I don't know. I think somebody got hit up."

"Why you say that?"

"'Cause I seen them putting yellow tape up."

"Where's the coke?"

"I got it. I was scared to death when I saw all the cops. I thought it was a setup."

"Did you see a green Suburban or a black Expedition?"

"As dirty as I was, I wasn't concentrating on nothing but getting the fuck out of harm's way."

Six was silent for a moment, trying to figure out what was going on. "Just put them bags in the garage for me before you go."

L got up and said, "A'ight."

"You can still knock off that two G's. You did your part."

"Word. Good look, Six."

* * *

"So he's yours?" Gee asked.

Manus sighed and nodded.

"Why do you seem so sad? You should be happy."

"'Cause I don't want no baby by that broad. She ain't right. Plus, some other stuff is bothering me."

"Well, I don't know what the other stuff is about, but I know that you have a responsibility and you should be happy."

"But look how long she's been keeping him from me. She should've been told me."

"Regardless of how she did it, you know now."

"But what I don't understand is why she all of a sudden wants me to be the daddy? She wasn't thinking about me when I was locked." Frustrated, Manus lay back on the couch and closed his eyes. He felt Gee slide closer to him.

She started massaging his temples. "Listen carefully. I understand how you must feel, as far as the situation about your son. But regardless of who the mother is, or what she's done to you in the past, you have to get into that little boy's life. It's not going to be easy, but if you allow another man to raise your son and you're able, it's going to assassinate your character."

"And you think I can do it?"

"The way you are there for me, I know you can."

Manus opened his eyes and looked at Gee. "I love the way that you believe in me. I love a lot of things about you." Manus raised up and kissed Gee passionately.

She pulled back. "I don't know how to kiss."

"Ain't nothing to it. Just follow my lead." Manus kissed her slowly and she caught on. The whole time, he caressed her breasts. This went on until his erection felt like it was about to burst. He pulled back. "What time do your roommate get off?"

Gee pulled her shirt over her head. "She's working late."

Manus did the same and laid her down on the couch.

She said, "You got a condom?"

"Yeah, but I don't need it just yet."

He went down on her and gasped when he saw that she was shaved completely bald.

Gee pulled him back up. "What are you doing?"

"Just relax." He went back down and spread her vagina open with his thumbs. Then he put her clitoris in his mouth and sucked it gently. He expertly maneuvered the tip of his tongue around it while he entered her with an index and a middle finger. Then he went to her inner thigh and began to tease it by licking and gently biting it.

Gee had never experienced this kind of pleasure before. Five minutes of it and she felt herself about to climax.

Manus noticed her squirming and started sucking vigorously on her clitoris.

As Gee climaxed she tried to back away from Manus, but he slid his arms under her thighs and locked his hands at her waist. A loud moan escaped her mouth. She straddled his head but didn't have the strength to apply pressure.

As she lay limp, Manus put on a condom and entered her.

Three minutes later Gee felt herself climaxing again.

*   *   *

Erica made the kids go to bed and went into the living room with Charles Sr. She sat beside him and said, "Charles, we got to talk."

He looked at her with an uninterested expression. "About what?"

"I ... I really don't know how to tell you this, but remember when we first got together?"

"Yeah. And?"

"Uh, remember I told you that I was depressed because my boyfriend just got locked up?"

"Yeah. And?"

"Well, I was depressed about something else, too."

"And what was that?" he asked, mugging her.

In a voice barely audible, she said, "'cause I was pregnant, too."

Charles leaned back. "So what are you saying?"

"That … that Lil' Charles ain't yours."

"What!"

Erica repeated herself.

"So who's the daddy?"

"My old boyfriend."

"Manus?"

Erica nodded.

"So you fucking played me?"

"It wasn't intentional. You were so happy when you found out, I ain't want to take that joy away from you."

"That's some bullshit. You ain't shit!" He got up and began to pace the floor.

"You're overreacting, Charles. At least I didn't take you on a talk show or nothing."

Charles stopped in his tracks and faced her. "What! Bitch, I should kill your ass. I've raised that boy as my own for seven years, and even though he don't got none of my features, I've never questioned you because I trusted you."

"Well, I'm sorry Charles. But my baby got the right to know who his biological father is."

"Don't act like it's all about the boy. I know you're going back to that nigga because his people got a lil' bread. I know all about that nigga."

"For one, I ain't going back to that nigga. And for two, why shouldn't my baby live the life if he can? Your broke ass can barely buy them a pair of shoes."

"Maybe if you help me pay some bills, I would have some extra money to get them what they need."

"And how the fuck am I suppose to help you pay the bills? I don't got a job."

"You get those checks."

"And?"

"Buying all that fake-ass hair and shit, you can use that money to help out."

"Anyway."

Charles shook his head and sighed. "My grandma told me not

to fuck with your trifling ass."

"Well, you should've listened to her. The only reason I fucked with your ass is because I thought you were a baller. Your broke ass ain't hitting on shit. I wish Kandis wasn't yours, either."

Something snapped in Charles's head and he rushed her. Erica tried to get away, but Charles rolled his hand up in her shirt and slapped her until his hand felt as though it would break.

*   *   *

A week later, Manus drove to the address that Six had given him. When he pulled up at the house in Strawberry Hills, he got out with his tool bag and knocked on the door.

"Who?" a man asked.

"It's Manus, Six's peoples."

When the door opened, a dark-skinned male observed Manus carefully. He was as tall as Manus but outweighed him by twenty pounds. He turned his head and yelled, "L, Six's peoples is here." Then he turned back to Manus. "Come on in, man."

Manus followed him through the neat house and into the kitchen. Two guys were standing over a pot, looking in it.

L looked up with lowered eyebrows, obviously frustrated. He shook Manus' hand and said, "What's going on? I'm L; that's Tee, and he's Rome."

Manus nodded at the men and said, "Manus."

L looked back at the pot and said, "That oil base is some bullshit. I hate fucking with it."

Manus looked in the pot. "What's going on with it?"

"It won't get hard for nothing. It's mad cut on it, ain't it?"

"I doubt it. Some oil base just needs more baking soda than others to get hard." Manus opened his tool bag and began to pull out all sorts of paraphernalia.

L said, "Now this is a man that's serious about his work."

Rome said, "Hell yeah."

L said, "Tee, go get my cigarettes in the living room."

When Tee returned with the cigarettes, Manus observed him for the first time. His small plaits that stuck straight up and his big eyes put Manus in the mind of a praying mantis. It was obvious from all of the scars on his face and hands that Tee had lived a rough life.

Manus turned the stove's eye on low and said, "How much coke in the pot?"

"A big eight."

Manus filled his Visionware pot halfway with water and set it on the eye. Then he weighed out an ounce of baking soda and put it in the pot. After that, he scraped the gooey oil base out of the other pot and into the Visionware glass pot. When the cocaine melted and floated to the top of the water, Manus took the pot off the eye and sprinkled cold water in it. When the cocaine sank to the bottom, he poured most of the water into a bowl. With the cake mixer, he began to blend the cocaine until it absorbed most of the remaining water. Waiting for this to happen, Manus ran a small amount of hot water in the pot and continued to blend it. He repeated the process two more times before he was satisfied. Five minutes later, he had a hard cookie of crack that weighed a little over seven ounces.

"Goddamn," L said. "You did your thing."

"I ain't through yet. It's still some coke left in the bowl."

L stroked his chin. "Look. I got two and a half that I was gonna move in soft, but the way you brought that back, I got to let you do them."

"Where they at?"

"Tee, go get them things out of the trunk." Then he said to Manus, "What do you call what you just did?"

"Water whip."

"Word. I like that shit. It looks easy."

"It is, but it's tricky, too."

"Yeah? Is it still some good, being that you got all that extra?"

"Yeah, I ain't overdo it."

After Manus cooked up the rest of the cocaine, he cleaned his tools and put them back into the bag. L paid him and said, "Can I get your number so I won't have to go through nobody to get up with you?" Manus gave him his number and left.

CHAPTER 12

"**D**id I tell you what I got planned for us tonight?" Manus asked Gee as they walked through Old Navy.

"I hope not too much because I need to go home to study for the upcoming exams."

"I made reservations at Karamas tonight. I guess we'll just skip the movies since you have to study."

"Sorry," Gee said sincerely.

"It's okay, I'll never get in the way of your schooling."

"Thank you."

Manus stopped the clothes cart at a rack that held velour sweatsuits.

"Ohh, this would look good on Lil' Charles."

"Yes, it would."

Manus looked for the right size and threw it in the cart with the rest of the clothes he was buying for his son.

Gee looked at him for a moment, but she remained silent.

Manus noticed the vibe and said, "What's wrong, baby?"

"Nothing really. I just noticed something."

"What's that?"

In a whisper she said, "Since I've been with you, I've noticed you spend money like you have an endless supply."

"I wish."

"But I can't tell that you don't. Look how you put that outfit in the cart without looking at the price tag."

She picked the suit up and looked at the price tag.

"This costs ninety-five dollars."

"That's not too bad."

"Look, Manus. I've tried to avoid the subject and wait for you to bring it up, but I see that's not going to happen. So instead of assuming, I'm just going to ask you what it is that you do?"

Manus took a deep breath and exhaled. He didn't feel comfortable talking to her about his career choice, but he didn't want to lie about it, either.

So far, their relationship had been smooth sailing, and he didn't want to see it any other way.

"I'm involved with drugs. But," he added quickly, "I don't deal them."

"I'm confused."

"How can I put this? Okay, I prepare it for the dealers but I don't deal them."

Gee gave him a sad look. "You know that I would love you the same if you didn't have money, right?"

"I know, baby. I know."

"Can you promise me one thing?"

"It depends on what it is."

"Can you promise me that you won't make the mistake into thinking that you can make a career out of that."

Manus thought about that. Then he thought about his goal, but at the same time, Grip's fears about the feds came to him. Manus knew that he wasn't trying to go back to prison.

At that moment, he decided that as soon as he could put the city on lock and get what he wanted out of it, he would move on to something else.

He hugged Gee, "I promise baby."

*   *   *

Tasha was a high yellow complexion with light brown hair. At five foot eight, she weighed a hundred and forty pounds. Her legs were so bowed that if they were straightened through a medical procedure, she would be nearly three inches taller. Her lips were the color of bubble gum, and when she spoke she revealed a perfect set of white teeth.

Tasha moaned as Meat toyed with her nipples, which were the same color as her lips. He knew what buttons to push to get her aroused. Tasha started breathing heavy and straddled Meat.

Meat had been with many women, but none of them could ride

like Tasha. She made him cross his legs and rode only the tip of his penis. Every ten seconds or so, she took all of him, but instantly came back to the tip. When she sensed that he was about to climax, she took all of him and switched to a grinding motion. This drove Meat crazy, but he kept his composure. He never showed his full emotions to women.

Meat was already upset with himself for going over his limit with Tasha. This made his fifth time having sex with her, the most he had ever been with one female.

After he climaxed, Tasha went down on him and took him in her mouth. She sucked the remainder of his flowing semen as she massaged his testicles. She pulled away and said, "Meat."

"What's up?"

"You know I love you, right?"

"Nah, I didn't know that."

"Well, I do."

"How do you know that you love me? I mean, what lets you know that you're in love with a person?"

"You know, just missing and wanting to be with that person all the time. It's a crazy but good feeling. But it's the best feeling when the person you're loving feels the same way."

"I feel that. But when is it a crazy feeling?"

"Hmm, I guess when the person that you're in love with don't love you, and/or they play with your feelings."

"I can go for that."

A moment passed before Tasha said, "So, how do you feel about me?"

"You cool."

"That's it?"

"To be honest with you, I really ain't the type that dwells on thoughts like that."

"Oh," she said solemnly. "So you're saying that because you haven't met the right person yet, or because you've been hurt before?"

"Neither. I was just taught by my cousin that that was the best way to be."

"Your cousin, huh?"

"Uh huh."

"So your cousin's a player, too?"

"Player? That word sounds like a person that's not in control."

"Well, your cousin be entertaining women, too?"

"Nah, not no more. He's married now." They started laughing.

Tasha said, "So he's plain proof that love can affect anybody."

"Of course. I wasn't saying that it was impossible for me to fall in love; I just said that I wasn't the type to entertain the thought."

"Oh. So how do you feel about babies?"

"Babies are cool. I don't have anything against them. They didn't ask to be here."

"That's what I told myself when I found out."

When it dawned on Meat, he said, "When you found out what?"

"That we're having a baby."

Meat sat up. "We, who?"

"Us. Me and you."

"Quit bullshitting."

Tasha reached on the floor and grabbed her pocketbook. She pulled out a used pregnancy test and handed it to Meat. He observed the test and said, "How I know it's mine? I know you and Gloria be doing y'all thing."

"For one," she said calmly, "You are the only nigga I fuck with, and that's on everything I love. For two, when I have it, we can get a blood test on the spot to clear all your doubts. I don't get down like that."

Meat stayed silent.

"So you mad?" Tasha asked.

After a moment passed, Meat said, "For what? The baby didn't ask to be here."

Tasha embraced him. "I was scared 'cause I thought you was gonna trip."

"Nah, everything's cool."

Tasha looked at him with a seductive look on her face. Meat recognized the look and said, "Oh no. I'm through."

"Through? What, you tired?"

"Nah, I got to go somewhere."

"Where you got to go?"

Meat looked at her and started to chastise her for questioning him, but he only said, "I'm going to the show."

"I thought you ain't club no more."

"I don't, but I'm tired of playing old man. I ain't been nowhere since I got shot."

Understanding, she said, "Well, I can stay here and wait for you?"

"I ain't gonna be back until around three or four."

"As long as you come back to me, I ain't tripping."

*   *   *

Fresh out of jail, Charles let himself in the apartment. Kandis looked up from playing with a baby doll and jumped up. "Daddy!"

Charles picked her up and kissed her. "My baby! You miss your daddy?"

"Yes. I been crying, too."

"Why have you been crying?"

"'Cause Momma won't let me go play outside with my friends."

Charles looked over at Erica who was hot curling her weave.

Then he looked back to Kandis. "Why your brother ain't take you outside?"

"'Cause he ain't here."

"He ain't?"

"No. He gone with his other daddy."

Charles felt a pang shoot through his chest and he sat Kandis down. "Well as soon as Daddy talks to Mommy, I'll take you outside. Okay?"

"Okay. Can we go to the store, too?"

"We sure can."

Kandis celebrated by jumping up and down while clapping.

"Now go upstairs until I finish talking to your momma."

"And then we going to the store and outside?"

"Yes, baby."

Kandis grabbed her babydoll from the floor and ran upstairs.

Charles looked at Erica and began walking toward her.

Erica held up the hot curlers. "You better not put your hands on me Charles."

"I'm not going to touch you; I just want to talk."

Erica looked at him suspiciously. "Alright, but I'm telling you."

Charles sat down beside her. "I can't believe that you done me dirty like that."

"I can't believe you beat me like that; I'm a woman."

"There's no excuse for that. I really do apologize." Charles reached to scratch his nose and Erica jumped. "God, Erica! I'm not going to hit you."

"Shit, I don't know."

A moment passed when Charles said, "I see that nigga been over here."

"He came to pick up Lil' Charles."

"Lil' Charles, huh?"

"What's that supposed to mean?" she asked with an attitude.

Charles ignored the question. "You been fucking that nigga while I was locked?"

"No, Charles. He haven't been in this house. He waited in the car."

Charles got up from the couch and kneeled on the floor. He took her free hand and tears began to form in his eyes. "Listen, baby. Do you really love me?"

"Don't ask me no crazy question like that."

"Please answer the question; I need to know."

"Yes, Charles, you know I love you."

"And can you honestly say that I've been a good father to both of the kids?"

Seeing where he was going with the conversation, Erica said, "Yes, you have been a decent father to the kids, but the fact remains that Lil' Charles needs to know his biological father."

"That dude ain't been there for that boy! I was there every time he got sick or needed something!"

"That's not fair. That man didn't even know he had a son. And plus, he was locked up."

"Fair? What about me? Is it fair that I have to endure this kind of shit?" Tears flowed rapidly down Charles's face.

Erica just turned her head away.

"Please, baby," Charles pleaded, "I just want us to be a family like we were."

"We still are a family."

"Well, can you just forget about that nigga then? I swear I'll step my game up. I swear!"

Erica looked at Charles for a long moment. She hated to see him like that, but she knew that her plans were bigger than his feelings. She wasn't about to let nothing get in her way, and that included Charles.

"I'm sorry, Charles. I can't do that."

Charles's bottom lip began to tremble. He jumped up to his feet and slammed the door as he went out!

*   *   *

Meat looked down at the gun lying on the passenger seat and shook his head. In his twenty-nine years of living, he had never carried a gun. But now it was a necessity. The night of the shooting replayed in his dreams every night. It was driving him mad. One particular incident that took place that night stood out like a sore thumb. He had kept his suspicions to himself. It was his own business to straighten, and nobody else's.

*   *   *

Meat paid the ridiculous price at the door and went into the club looking like a million dollars. His mood instantly changed when his cousin's words came to him. *If you want to attract the broads, first of all, you got to dress the flyest you can. Illusion gets them every time. But the trick is, you got to act oblivious to the attention you're getting. Women can't stand a man that's stuck on himself. The most important thing that you got to remember, every move that you make has to be gradual and casual. Don't never seem too eager to do anything.*

As Meat moved through the crowd, males and females admired the all-white Fendi outfit that he sported. He looked straight ahead with a relaxed face. It brought out his features better — let his cousin tell it. By the time he reached the bar and ordered a bottle of Moët, a group of women filled in the stools around him.

Glancing at the cutest one on his right, he admired the come-fuck-me outfit that she wore. He decided right then that Tasha would have to wait a little longer tonight.

It was obvious that he wanted to say something to her, but he held back. It wasn't his style to make introductions. The pleasure was all theirs.

The woman finally gave in and leaned toward him. "Excuse me, what's your name?"

Meat casually took a sip from the bottle and let a few seconds pass before saying, "Meat."

"Meat, you killing them with that outfit."

"Thank you. You too," he said humbly.

She extended her hand. "I'm Ebony."

Meat shook her hand. "Nice to meet you, Ebony."

"You can't be from Raleigh, 'cause I would know you. Or would have at least seen you before."

"Nah, I'm from Durham."

Another woman said, "You from Durham? I know you got some weed or something. I don't fuck around with that heroin."

"Me either. I got them jump-offs, though."

The women got excited and said to the others, "Girl, he got those thangs!"

Ebony said, "How much you letting them go for?"

"Two-five. They them triple stack Nikes."

"Can I get one for twenty?"

"Depends."

"On what?"

"On who you leaving with when it kicks in."

All the women began to giggle. One wearing a Coogi dress said, "You got some more friends like you here?"

When Meat turned his attention to Coogi dress, Ebony grabbed his arm and said, "I'm leaving with you."

CHAPTER 13

Tee tapped L on the shoulder. "There go your boy."

L saw Manus standing near the bar and waved him over.

Manus walked up and gave the men some dap.

"What's going on?" L asked.

"Chilling, chilling."

"If I would've known you were coming, I would've had you ride with us."

"I ain't even know. It was a spur-of-the-moment thing."

"You smoke? I got some blue berry."

"Nah, I don't fuck around."

"Come on, at least let me buy you a drink."

"Word."

The men went over to the bar and ordered drinks. They were in general conversation when they noticed a crowd of women gathered around a guy in all white. Assuming that one of the featured artists had come to get a drink, Rome said, "That nigga down here without bodyguards? He *can't* have no jewels on."

"He better not," Tee said, as he walked over there.

L said to Manus, "That nigga always on the prowl."

Manus raised his eyebrows and shrugged.

Tee came back with an evil grin on his face. "Yo, that's ole boy."

"Who?"

"Meat."

"Meat? Meat? I've heard that name somewhere before," Manus said.

L said, "Probably have. He ain't nobody but a fronting-ass nigga."

"What, y'all got beef or something with him?"

"I wouldn't call it beef but, let him tell it, he be flaming at us every time he sees us."

"And ain't popped one shell, have he?" Manus asked.

"Hell nah."

"Stunting." Manus looked in Meat's direction again.

Rome, L, and Tee simultaneously said, "Exactly."

Everybody's attention turned to the stage when a featured artist began to perform.

* * *

As Meat watched the performance, someone tapped him on the shoulder.

Coogi dress said, "Meat, what's up?"

"Nothing. What's up with you?"

"Nothing. I just wanted to introduce myself. I'm Star."

"Nice to meet you, Star."

She smiled and said, "Likewise." Then she said, "I was just over there with Ebony."

"How could I forget?"

The smile again. "Look, I want you to take my number so we can get up."

Meat took the piece of paper.

Then she said, "Yeah, you don't want to fuck with Ebony. She melts condoms."

"Yeah?"

"Yeah, that bitch is nasty."

"I'm glad you told me."

"I had to. But look, holla at me whenever."

"I will."

Meat turned toward the stage and felt someone bump him from behind. When the guy passed him, Meat's eyes got as big as saucers when he saw that it was L. He quickly regained his composure and said, "Better watch where the fuck you going!"

Rome, Tee, and Manus arrived as L said, "A'ight now. Don't get that pretty lil' outfit stomped out."

"Whatever, nigga. You gonna need all your do-boys, 'cause I will punish you."

Tee stepped up and said, "Who the fuck you calling a do-boy?"

"Man, you better get the fuck out my face!"

Tee dropped his drink and threw up his guards.

L grabbed him and said, "Chill." Then he said to Meat, "The best thing you can do is burn out. Go put some flowers on your man's grave or something." Before L knew what was happening, Meat had swung the Moët bottle at his head.

Manus swiftly swatted Meat's wrist with so much force, the bottle came out of his hand. Before Manus could make another move, the men were all over Meat. Manus just stepped back. Twenty seconds later, security came and began to toss the men every which way. Even a few women got tossed aside.

*   *   *

"Can't none of you pussy niggas fight!" Meat screamed. "Tell the police to take the cuffs off and let us do straight fades. I'll drag all y'all niggas!"

L said, "Shhh! Quit talking in front of the man. You don't really want to fight; you trying to get saved by going to jail."

"I don't see you, L. And now I know you had something to do with Brad. It's on. That's my word!"

L looked at Rome. "You hear that nigga?"

"I heard him. He straight police."

A white officer with blond hair intervened. "All you guys better shut up before I charge you with being drunk and disorderly. The magistrate on duty tonight will hold you in the drunk tank for twenty-four hours."

Those simple words would calm the men down. Short speeches like that were just as crucial.

The officer then saw Manus standing at the entrance. "You better go back inside before you find yourself in a pair of cuffs also." Manus looked at the police and then back to Meat before walking back to the dance area.

Uncuffing Meat, the officer said, "Are you okay?"

"They ain't do shit."

"Do you want to press charges?"

Meat glared at L and shook his head no.

"Now, I'm going to give you a five-minute head start. But after that, you're on your own." Meat took one last look at L before walking through the lobby doors.

After the three men were uncuffed, the officer said, "Usually we take you guys to jail for fighting, but because the other party didn't want to press charges and handled his own, we decided to turn you guys loose."

Tee said, "He ain't do shit but get his ass whipped!"

The officer said, "Especially you. Look at your eye." Tee touched his eye and felt a lump the size of a hot ball.

The cops started laughing. They let five minutes pass before they turned the men loose. The white officer said, "Stop at the store and get your friend some ice for his eye."

Tee stopped and turned around. "Fuck you, you fat-ass cracker!"

"A hundred percent cracker. Wouldn't have it no other way."

"If it wasn't for that badge —"

"Come on," L said, grabbing his arm. "He trying to trap you off."

"Muthafuckin cracker trying to play me. Man, I swear to God!"

A young black officer that had been humble throughout the whole ordeal approached L and said, "Get your man out of here before he goes to jail. He don't need no bullshit-ass charge."

"I got him. I got him."

L and Rome escorted Tee to the car and put him in. When they were all in, L said, "Crazy-ass night."

Rome said, "Hell yeah."

"That nigga almost took my head off with that bottle."

"Yeah, that chef nigga saved your ass. You better call that nigga and thank him."

"Think I ain't? I'mma call him first thing in the morning."

Rome looked in the back seat and saw that Tee was holding his eye. "You a'ight?"

"Yo, I'mma kill that nigga. I'm talking about a walk up; he won't survive this one."

"You already know, so don't stress it."

Now that Meat's fate had been decided, Tee felt a little better. He began to relax. "I can't even front; though, that nigga hit harder than a muthafucka."

The men started laughing.

L said, "Did y'all peep how them hoes tried to help that nigga?

One of them hoes scratched me on the neck."

Tee said, "Hell yeah. One bitch in a Coogi dress tried to kick me in the nuts."

"Yeah?"

"And I tried to break her jaw."

Rome said, "Was them hoes from Durham?"

"I don't know, but if you see a thick, dark-skinned bitch with a wired-up jaw, that's her." The men laughed.

L stopped at a convenience store for a blunt. Rome got out, too. Tee rolled down his window. "L, get me a bag of Doritos."

"Nigga, I ain't your maid. You better get out and get it yourself."

Tee looked in the store and saw several women. "Come on, man. I can't go in there around all them hoes with my eye looking like this."

L looked in the store. Then he looked back in the car and saw that Tee's eye was nearly swollen shut. "A'ight, man, I got you."

"And get me some ice." Tee tilted his head back and closed his eyes. He ached as if he were the one that had gotten jumped on. All he wanted right now was a hot shower and some sleep.

When Tee opened his eyes to see what was taking them so long, he saw a figure walking toward the car. The hooded sweatshirt concealed the figure's identity.

Now, five feet from the car, the figure pulled a semi-automatic handgun from the pocket of the sweatshirt and aimed at Tee.

Tee scrambled to the other side of the seat and tried to get out. As he opened the door, the gunman fired two shots, striking Tee's shoulder once.

Tee fell out of the car and hit the ground. He got up and took off running. The gunman easily caught up with him and shot him three times in the back. By the time Tee's body hit the ground, the killer was already running back to a getaway car.

*   *   *

Lauren was awakened by the ringing of the phone. "Hello?" She heard someone crying on the other end of the phone. "Hello?" she said again.

"I'm so sorry, Lauren. I … I'm so sorry for making your life … so miserable," Brian sobbed.

"How dare you call me at this time of the night! How dare you call me at all, you low-down, dirty bastard!"

"You won't have to worry about me anymore after tonight."

Lauren was about to hang up, but she noticed something disturbing in his voice.

Then he said, "Brad didn't deserve to die; it should've been me instead. I ... I should've been a better father."

Lauren felt absolutely no sympathy for him. Once again she wanted to hang up, but something in his voice made her stay on the phone. "Brian, are you drunk?" Silence.

"Hello?" She finally heard a gunshot.

*   *   *

When the gunshots went off, everybody in the store hit the floor.

Ten seconds later, a woman came running in the store screaming, "Oh my God! Oh my God! Somebody call the ambulance; a man just got shot!"

Rome and L jumped off the floor and ran outside. The first thing they saw was the shattered window of L's Lexus.

Both men stopped running and walked around the car slowly. Forty yards from the car, they saw Tee lying facedown on the pavement. They rushed up to their friend. Rome was about to turn him over, but L stopped him.

"No, don't move him!" L knelt down to Tee's face. "Tee! Tee! Talk to me, man!"

Rome stood and began pacing back and forth.

"Goddamn!"

A crowd started to gather around. Some were mumbling and some were crying.

L looked up at them. "What are ya'll just standing there for? Somebody call the muthafucking ambulance!"

One woman said, "We already did."

Screaming at the top of his lungs, L said, "Well call them again, goddamnmit!"

Rome saw that L was losing control, so he stepped to him.

"Chill, L. He's gone."

"Nah, man, I seen him move."

"L, he's gone."

L stared at Tee's lifeless body. Tears began to run down his face.

"That nigga killed my man. That coward nigga killed my man."

A woman pushed her way through the crowd and stopped dead in her tracks when she saw L kneeling over Tee's body.

"Oh my God," she said putting her hands over her mouth. "L, where's Rome? Please!"

Rome heard his son's mother's voice and turned around.

"Renee."

Renee looked and ran into Rome's arms. "Thank God!" Then she said, "What happened?"

"I don't know."

"It had to be Mea —"

Rome put his hand over her mouth. "Shh."

From a distance, sirens could be heard.

Rome suddenly remembered the guns that were in the car. "Come with me."

Renee followed Rome to L's Lexus.

Rome quickly retrieved the pistols. When he only found two, he realized that Tee had his gun on him. Getting out the car with the guns wrapped in a T-shirt, Rome said, "Hurry up; take these to your car."

Renee grabbed the shirt and hurried to her car. No sooner than she got to her car, two police cruisers pulled up.

Rome swore under his breath when he saw that they were the same officers that had detained them at the club.

CHAPTER 14

Denise handed her friend Keisha three photos and said, "Here they go right here."

Keisha stared at the pictures. "Damn, girl! Pat is fine as hell. Look at his muscles."

Denise smiled proudly, "Yeah, he done got so big. I told him that them hoes going to be tearing his clothes off when he gets out."

Still looking at the pictures, Keisha just shook her head.

"Ain't no telling what I'll do to him if I get a hold of him." The phone started ringing and Denise answered it, "Hello."

When she heard the automated voice she said, "This is him right here." Denise accepted the call and said, "Hello?"

"What's up, sis?" Pat asked.

"Hey, boy. We was just talking about you."

"You and Ma?"

"Nah, me and Keisha."

"You talking about little Keisha from across the street?"

"She ain't little no more. She's a grown woman now."

"Let me holla at her right quick."

"Hold on." She gave the phone to Keisha. "My brother wants to talk to you."

Seconds later, Keisha got on the phone. "Hello?"

"What's up?"

"You."

"Yeah?"

"Uhm-hmm."

"My sister told me that you're grown now."

"Thick and all."

"Send a nigga some flicks then, so I can confirm that."

"What kind do you want?"

"What kind are you gonna take?"

"Whatever kind you can have in there."

Pat grabbed his crotch through his khakis. "Damn, you gangster like that?"

"I'm a rider."

"You got a man?"

"Yeah, but he's sorry as hell."

"So can you send me some lingerie shots?"

"Yeah. Do you got any preferred poses or positions."

"Sheeitt, just make sure I can see that pussy print good."

"Oh, you going to see it. I guarantee."

"When I get your flicks, I'll send you some of me."

"I'm looking at some now. You look edible."

Pat squeezed himself harder. "I am; I swear to God I am."

"So when are you getting out?"

"Uh, in a minute. I got some legal issues in the courts right now that should set me free," he lied.

"I'll pray for you."

"Thank you."

"Are you coming to stay with your mom when you get out?"

"Up until I get my shit together. Why you ask?"

"'Cause I want to be the first one to see your ass so I can put it on you."

"If you act right while I'm in here, you'll be the only one putting it on me when I get out."

"You ain't said nothing; I told you I'm a rider."

"Look, make sure you get my address from my sister."

"I will."

"And don't forget about the flicks."

"I won't."

"I'll write you as soon as I get them. Let me holla back at Denise."

"Okay, bye."

"Bye."

Denise got back on the phone. "What's up?"

"Hey, sis, make sure you give Keisha my address."

"I will. I'll do it as soon as I hang up with you."

"Good look. Where's Momma?"

"Sleep."

"She been a'ight?"

"Yeah, a lot better than before."

"Tell her I called, and I love her."

"I will."

"So, what's been going on out there?"

"Not — Oh, your mans was fighting at the Ritz last night."

"Who, Manus?"

"Yep, that's what I heard."

"Who was he fighting?"

"I didn't hear who, but I heard that somebody from Durham got killed at the store up the street from the club."

"You don't know who?"

"Hold on."

He heard her ask Keisha.

She got back on the phone and said, "Keisha said it was a nigga named Tee."

"You sure it wasn't Manus?"

"Yeah. I just passed him a lil' while ago. He was pushing a Camry."

Pat exhaled with relief, "Word. Look, let me go. I'll catch up with you later."

"A'ight."

"And don't forget to give Keisha my address."

"I won't."

"Bye." Pat hung up the phone thinking about Keisha. When he turned from the phone, he didn't see the newcomer until they almost collided.

Frowning, the newcomer said, "About time you got off."

Pat looked at the man for a long moment before walking away. His mind was on other things.

In the day room, Pat sat in front of the TV trying to picture what Keisha looked like now. He remembered her as being a cute girl, but because she was his sister's age, five years younger than him, he had never paid much attention to her. He couldn't wait to get the pictures. When he recalled the conversation that he'd had with Keisha, he remembered her asking him when was he was getting out of prison. In reality, that was a question for which he had no answer. It was a question that haunted and tormented him every day. As quick as his spirits had been lifted they'd been grounded. He knew he had to get out.

As he watched 106 and Park, he fiended on Free in the tight jeans that she wore. Ever since he had seen her do the Cat Woman crawl with Halle Berry, he had been infatuated with her.

From behind him, he heard someone say, "The joint that I came from watched the news around this time. Y'all dumb-ass niggas watching that BET shit need to turn your radios to a rap station if you want to hear that shit."

The same newcomer from the phone walked past Pat and turned the TV to the news.

Pat was so shocked that he was unable to speak.

A few people who had been watching BET complained, but the large newcomer muted them with a stare. Pat got over his shock, got up, and changed the TV back to BET.

"What the fuck are you doing?" asked the newcomer.

"I'm turning the shit back. I don't know how it was where you came from, but you got it fucked up if you think that you just gonna come in here and turn shit. Especially while I'm watching it."

The newcomer gave Pat a menacing look. "Fuck you and whatever you was watching."

With that said, the newcomer went back to the TV and reached up to change it.

As soon as Free disappeared from the screen, Pat charged the newcomer. He locked him in the half nelson and rammed his head against the wall.

The newcomer sank to the floor — unconscious.

All of Pat's worries and frustrations came out, and he beat the newcomer until the correction officers arrived and pulled him off.

*   *   *

Manus sat in his used Camry and counted out all the money that he had to his name. Eight hundred dollars. He wondered what was going on with Six, who hadn't called him for a job in a week.

He looked at Erica's apartment complex and blew the horn. This would be the first time being alone with his son.

When they came out, Lil' Charles jumped in the passenger side and Erica shut the door.

Manus looked at her and said, "A'ight then."

"Hold up. Let me holla at you for a minute." She walked around to his side, and Manus lowered his window two inches.

"What's up?"

"Get out, man. I ain't gonna bite."

Manus got out and shut the door. He noticed the fading bruises on her face.

"Yeah, he beat my ass when I told him, but his ass went to jail for it, too."

Manus didn't respond.

Erica said, "So what y'all gonna do?"

"I don't know yet."

"So, how's your girlfriend treating you?"

"Man, I'll holla. I'll have him back by five."

"Take my number in case something happens."

"Your number? Thought you ain't have a phone?"

"I was just trying to respect Charles, but fuck him now. I'm a free agent."

Manus stored the number in his phone and got back inside the car. As he did, he saw Shawnda standing behind the screen door. Manus pulled off and glanced down at Lil' Charles. *What am I supposed to say?* Manus thought. They rode in silence until Lil' Charles said, "Where we going?"

"Where you want to go?"

"I don't care."

"You hungry?"

"No," Charles said.

Manus guessed that Lil' Charles was as nervous as he was. He decided to make things easier. "I'll tell you what. Let's just go to the mall and play some games, and if we get hungry afterward, we'll get something to eat. Okay?"

"Okay."

* * *

"What do you think?" the detective asked the white officer.

"Those fucking guys are lying; I know it. I saw the hostility in those guys' eyes before I released them, and you could tell that their confrontation was more than a club brawl. It was something close and personal."

"That's the impression that I got also."

"I say we go back in there and play hardball with them sons of bitches."

"That's not a bad idea."

The detective and the officer left the room and headed for the two interrogation rooms. They stopped at the first door and the uniformed officer said, "Which one do you want to go at first?"

The detective thought about the question for a moment, then he said, "Let's try the emotional one first, he looks like he's about to crack at any moment."

They entered the second door.

L lay with his head buried in the cradle of his arms. When the door opened, he looked up and stared with blood-shot eyes.

"Mr. Beasley, how are you doing?" the detective asked.

"Man, when the fuck are y'all gonna let me go? I've been here about ten hours answering the same fucking questions."

"We're going to keep you here until you tell us the truth."

"I told you the truth a hundred fucking times. What, y'all want me to make up something?"

"We just want you to tell us the name of the guy that you guys were fighting at the club."

"I said I didn't know, goddamnmit!"

The white officer pointed a finger real close to L's face, "You better watch your mouth, boy, before you be picking it up off the floor."

"The only kind of boy I know is a cowboy and a white boy and I ain't either one of them, so you better watch your finger!"

"Before you get me killed like you got your boy killed tonight?"

"You're talking real stupid now."

The detective said, "Yeah, Mr. Beasley. Your boy Romel Bass just gave up the goods on you."

"Yeah, right."

"No, I'm serious. He wrote a statement on you and we released him."

The white officer said, "So it's over for you, unless you give us the name of the guy that you were fighting."

L looked at them both and smiled.

The policemen just looked at each other.

When L's smile receded, he said, "Y'all muthafuckas need to go back to academy school with that weak-ass game. Matter of fact, I don't got shit else to say to y'all. Either charge me with something or let me the fuck go."

The officer and the detective looked at one another, knowing it was time to try their luck with Rome.

*   *   *

Rome burst out laughing. "Man, y'all muthafuckas are crazy. I didn't have shit to do with that. When y'all gonna let me go?"

"You might not be going home for a while."

"Picture that."

"I'm serious, Mr. Bass. Evidently you don't know the law very well. If the investigating officer, which in this case is me, has reason to believe that a possible witness is withholding murder evidence, he can in fact charge conspiracy to commit murder, aiding and abetting — the list goes on, Mr. Bass."

The white officer stepped up and said, "It's up to you now."

Rome looked at the men and burst out laughing again. "Y'all muthafuckas are hilarious. Oh shit!"

The detective said, "Mr. Bass, this isn't a joking matter. A man, your alleged friend, has just been murdered, and you don't want to help us get his killer? Something is seriously wrong with this picture."

"The only thing that is seriously wrong is my ass still here. I have told y'all all that I know, but you still insist that I'm lying. So, now, I'm tired of y'all shit. I don't have shit to say no more." Rome held his wrists up to the detective. "Handle your business or let me go."

*　　　*　　　*

L walked out of the police station and shielded his eyes from the rays of the sun. Ten feet away he saw Rome, his back turned, smoking a cigarette.

L walked to him and placed a hand on his shoulder. "You good?"

Rome turned around and the men embraced. "Yeah, I'm good."

L studied the clouds with a distant look in his eyes. "I can't believe this shit. Man, I swear to God!"

Rome took a long toke from the cigarette and threw it down. After blowing the smoke out he said, "I can't believe this shit, either. I know Tee's momma is flipping out. And today's her birthday."

"Wherever I see that nigga at, it's going down. It can be at the mall, the courthouse, or wherever. I don't give a fuck!"

After a few minutes passed, Rome said, "What the fuck they do with your car?"

"They're holding it until tomorrow. They talked about the forensic people ain't finish with it."

"Damn, how the fuck are we going to get home? Cab?"

"Nah, Gloria's on the way. She's been up here since last night waiting."

"Word."

For the next ten minutes neither man said a word. They thought about Tee and what they were obligated to do when they got back to Durham. So when Gloria pulled up, they got into the car with one thing on their minds. Seek and destroy.

CHAPTER 15

After playing games in the arcade for two hours, Manus and Lil' Charles had built up an appetite. At Lil' Charles' request, they ate steak hoagies and fries at Steak Express. Manus looked across the table at the boy whom he was rapidly becoming attached to. When he thought about all the years of Lil' Charles' life that he had missed, he felt a strong hatred for Erica. He also hated her for letting another man reap the pleasures of fathering his son. He wondered how long it would take for Lil' Charles to accept him as his father.

Lil' Charles brought him out of his daze. "Since you my real daddy, do I got to change my name to Matthew Parrish, Jr.?"

Manus grinned. "Only if you want to."

"I don't know. I got to think about that one."

Manus laughed.

"Do I have to call you *Daddy*?"

"It's like this. I'm your dad, but I want you to see me as a good friend. You can talk to me about anything. I'm never going to tell you what to do, but I'll always give you some strong advice. I've been your age before, so I know I'll be able to relate to a lot of things that you might go through." Manus paused to eat a fry. "Right now, I know that it's gonna take some time for you to get used to me. Shee — Shoot, I got to get used to being a daddy. But I will, and I promise to always be there for you. Okay?"

"Okay."

"Now let's finish eating. I seen these shoes that would look good on you."

*   *   *

The detective handed Lauren a cup of coffee and sat back down at his desk.

"Thank you."

"No problem. How are you holding up?"

"I'm okay. This has been a tragic year for me."

"I know, and I'm sorry, too."

Lauren nodded.

"Tell me this, Ms. Taylor. Other than your son's death, why would your ex-husband kill himself?"

"To be honest with you, Detective, I don't think my son's death played a role in Brian's suicide. I think he just wanted me to think it did."

"Why do you say that?"

"Because he was broke and on a guilt trip. He used to have a pawn shop, but he got busted for buying and selling stolen goods."

"Yes, I saw that on his rap sheet."

"And after that, his second wife left him and took his house."

The detective wrote something down. Then he said, "How did he react to Bradley's death?"

"As usual, he was thinking about himself."

"What do you mean by that?"

Lauren frowned. "Not only did that bastard skip my son's funeral, but he had the audacity to show up at my house a month later and ask for half of Bradley's insurance policy."

"Oh my."

"So you can see that Brian and I wasn't on the best of terms prior to his death."

"I understand. I would like to thank you for your time, Ms. Taylor," the detective said as he stood.

Lauren stood also and allowed the detective to lead her out of his office. When she got to the hallway, she saw Bobby with his head down. He appeared to be crying. Lauren felt guilty for not being affected by Brian's death. She walked over and hugged him.

*   *   *

Shawnda rode slowly by the house, but she did not see Grip's Range Rover parked there this time. "Damn, baby, where are you?" She picked up speed in her gold Honda Civic.

As she drove farther up the street, a 300M Chrysler passed by her. Shawnda watched from her side mirror as the car turned in the driveway of the house she had just watched.

"Bingo," Shawnda said as she whipped into someone's driveway to turn around.

When she got back to the house, she pulled into the driveway behind the Chrysler. A few seconds later, a brown-skinned woman got out of the car, carrying shopping bags and talking on the phone. She looked at Shawnda and walked toward the car. In a very polite voice she said, "May I help you with something?"

Shawnda observed the nice-figured woman's Chanel dress and matching heels. On her neck, she sported a solitary diamond and platinum necklace. Shawnda hated her. "Yes, you can. I'm looking for Grip."

The lady frowned and then said in the phone, "Hey, girl, let me call you when I get in the house … Bye." She ended the call and said, "Excuse me; Grip doesn't live here, and I would appreciate it if you didn't come back here."

"Well, I'd *appreciate* if you would give me his number because I got to talk to him."

"Whatever business you may have with Grip, please don't involve me in it."

"Well, if you give me his number, I won't have to involve your ass no more!"

"I'm sure that if Grip wanted you to have his number, then he would have given it to you. Now, please leave."

The lady turned away and began walking toward the house.

Shawnda stuck her head out the window and yelled, "Bitch, you ain't all that. That's why he's playing your dumb ass!"

The lady waved her off. "Child, I'm a grown woman. I don't have time for your mess."

"I'll kick your ass, you anorexic-looking-ass bitch!"

The lady entered her house and closed the door.

Shawnda put the car in reverse and waited for the traffic to allow her out. She focused on the parked Chrysler and wanted to ram it. She dismissed the thought; she remembered that she didn't have any car insurance.

*   *   *

Manus grabbed the bag that Lil' Charles had forgotten and took it to the door. Erica seemed to be waiting for them because she had opened the door as soon as they pulled up.

Lil' Charles screamed, "Where's Kandis? He bought her some shoes, too!" He stepped inside.

Manus, too, stepped inside and gave him the bag.

Lil' Charles disappeared up the stairs.

Erica said, "Thank you."

"It's nothing."

Erica held her short silk robe closed. "Have a seat. Want something to drink or something?"

"Nah, I'm good. I got to go."

Kandis came down the stairs full speed. "Momma! Look at my new shoes Manus bought me!"

"What do you say?"

"Thank you, Manus."

"You're welcome."

When Lil' Charles came back downstairs, he was wearing his new shoes. He walked over to Manus and gave him a hug. "Thank you. I had a good time."

"You're welcome. I had a good time, too. See you later, okay?"

"Okay." Then he turned to Kandis, "Come on, let's go play the game." The kids disappeared up the stairs.

Manus said to Erica, "A'ight then, I'll holla."

Just as Shawnda had instructed her, Erica let her robe fall open.

Manus took one look at her naked body and headed out the door.

"What, you don't like women no more?"

"It ain't that. I don't hit just anything no more."

*   *   *

When Manus got outside, he saw a gold Honda Civic parking beside his car. Shawnda got out of the Civic and paused. "Hey, Manus."

Manus nodded and kept walking to his car.

Once he was in the Camry, Shawnda tapped on the passenger window.

"Goddamn," Manus mumbled. He lowered the window a few inches and stared at her.

"Are you okay?" she asked.

Manus frowned. "What are you talking about?"

"I heard that y'all were fighting Meat at the Ritz last weekend. I ain't know you fuck with L and them like that."

"That was *them* niggas fighting."

"Well, I'm glad Meat ain't shoot you, too. I really can't blame him, though. I would've done the same thing if they would've shot me and killed my best friend."

"Huh?"

"Yeah, you ain't know that Meat was beefing with L and them? Meat's friend Brad got killed in that beef." The expression on Manus' face told Shawnda that he never knew. She said, "Yeah, you better be careful. You walked in on a war."

"'Preciate it. I got to go."

"Hey, can I get Grip's number? I got to ask him something real important."

"Shawnda, you know I can't give out that man's number like that."

"I figured that," she said, handing him a piece of paper. "Just tell him to call me."

"A'ight." Manus cranked his car and pulled off. Up until now, Manus thought his ears had deceived him in the lobby of the club. But now it was clear to him, and so was what he had to do.

*   *   *

When Shawnda entered the apartment, she took one look at Erica and knew that something was bothering her. "Bitch, you must've gotten about as much accomplished as I got with Grip."

"Girl, I think he's gay or something."

"Did you do it exactly like I told you to do it?"

"Girl, I flung my robe back so hard, it looked like a cape blowing back."

"He seen your goods and all?"

"Everything but the bottom of my feet."

"Damn, bitch, don't feel bad. At least you came in contact with him. I couldn't even find Grip's ass. That house I told you I seen his truck at, I went there and bumped heads with one of his bitches."

"For real?"

"For real."

"Tell me you didn't show out."

"Bitch, you know I did."

Erica started laughing and got comfortable on the couch.

"Girl, give me the whole scoop."

Shawnda sat down. "I seen the bit —"

"Ma!" Lil' Charles yelled, running down the stairs. "Kandis won't give me my shoe back."

"Boy, I don't want to hear that shit! Your ass been gone all day and it's been peaceful. Now take your ass back upstairs; don't you see grown folks are talking?"

Lil' Charles marched back up the stairs, mumbling under his breath.

Shawnda took five minutes to fill Erica in on all that had recently happened.

Shaking her head, Erica said, "This shit is a trip, ain't it? Eight years ago, I would have never thought that I'll be the one chasing a man."

"Yeah, bitch. We're getting old and fat. Our pussies don't be getting wet like them young girls. That's why when we hook a man, we got to juice his ass dry before he lose interest."

Now that Erica knew that there was no chance of hooking Manus, she started thinking of a way to juice him dry.

*   *   *

Manus pulled up in the Fayetteville Street projects and got out. When he got to the apartment door and raised his hand to knock, he paused when he heard someone inside arguing.

Just then, the door opened and a woman came out stomping. "Sorry-ass nigga. I knew you wasn't ready for no relationship. I played my own self by fucking back with you." She shoved Manus as she passed him. "Get out of my way, faggot."

A man came to the door, yelling, "I wish I *would* attempt to make a housewife out of ... Oh shit! Manus!" The men embraced.

"What's the deal, Wheat?"

"Not shit. Maintaining. Come in, nigga, before the police ride by."

Manus followed him into the apartment and saw *The Bronx Tale* on TV. Manus said, "I love this movie."

"Yeah, that's my shit. I watch it every day."

Manus observed Wheat in the wife beater. "I see you ain't lost it."

"Nothing major. Just something to keep a nigga off me," he said, flexing his muscles. The men laughed. Then he said, "Polar told me you were home."

"Yeah, I ain't too long touched down."

"Seeing you here can't be a good thing. Last time you was here, you was all in the paper for touching a nigga."

"Yeah, that was some bullshit."

"Man, you know I ain't judging you. Fuck that other nigga." The men bumped fists. "What's up, though? Holla at me."

"Yo, I need something with a lot of digits, but my money is funny."

"Something big?"

"Nah, something small."

"I'll be right back." Wheat disappeared up the stairs and came back a minute later. Keep your money. This is my welcome-home present." He handed Manus a Glock 9 handgun.

CHAPTER 16

The phone rang six times before Manus turned over and answered it. Once he heard that it was a collect call from prison, he immediately sat straight up. After accepting the call and waiting for the line to click through, Manus said, "Hello?"

"Man, what's the deal?" Pat said.

"Nigga, why you ain't been calling me?"

"I just got out the hole."

"For what?"

"For serving this new nigga for trying to turn the TV."

"For real? Man, you need to lay back. Did you get the flicks and bread I sent you?"

"Yeah, I got it. 'Preciate it."

"It's nothing."

"I was going to write back, but these crackers in here got real-live grimy on me. They wouldn't let me have shit in the hole but soap and my shower shoes."

"Damn, you got to chill."

"It's hard. My sister told me you copped a Camry and shit."

"It's old. Just something to get around in."

"Plus I heard about some shit that popped off with you in the club. What's up?"

"I mean, some shit did pop off, but I wasn't really involved. It's a whole lot of crazy shit going on. I just wish I could talk to you face to face."

"You got to wait six months before you can come and see me."

"I know. It's so much going on, that by the time six months is up, it'll take about ten visits to fill you in."

"Ain't nothing wrong with that. You good, though?"

"I'm good."

"Hey, so that's your girl you're hugged up with in the picture?"

"Yeah, that's her."

Pat was silent for a moment, then he said, "Yo, I got to get out of this muthafucka. I don't know how much longer I can hold on."

"Quit talking crazy; you're going to get out."

"My mom talked to this big-time lawyer in Charlotte, and he reviewed my case. He told her that there's so many inconsistencies in my case, and if she pay him twenty G's, he says he can get me out."

"Yeah? How much do your mom got so far?"

Pat sighed. "My mom is sick, dog. She haven't worked in five years."

"Will the lawyer take payments?"

"My mom said he will, but he wants fifteen thousand up front."

"Goddamn! That's the whole thing just about."

"I know, man. That cracker don't trust a soul."

"Faggot-ass nigga."

Pat was silent.

Manus said, "Just lay back and chill; everything's going to fall in place."

"I'm tired of laying back. I swear if I start really believing that I ain't going to never get out again, these muthafuckas in here are going to be in trouble. And I ain't talking about the inmates, either."

*　　*　　*

L and Rome had searched the city for a week straight, looking for Meat, but couldn't find him anywhere. L grieved for Tee, but more than anything his pride was hurt. He was a strong believer that a crew was as strong as its weakest link. For his circle to be penetrated by a nonviolent playboy like Meat, it made him look bad. He knew that everybody was laughing at him, and it was more than he could bear.

*　　*　　*

Manus drove through the Strawberry Hills neighborhood to see if L's car was home. As he did, he saw Rome walking from his car. Rome spotted him and flagged for him to stop.

Manus knew that it would seem odd if he kept going, so he stopped. When he got out, Rome walked up and bumped fists with him.

"What's the deal?"

"Chilling, chilling."

"We been trying to get up with you, but L lost his phone in the club that night."

"Yeah?"

"Hell yeah. Come in, man. L's in the house."

Manus observed his surroundings and didn't see anyone in sight. He figured that he had a good chance of handling his business and getting away clean. He looked down at his shirt to make sure that the gun wasn't bulging.

"Yo, L. Look who I found."

L looked up from a book called *Court in the Streets*. He saw Manus and stood to shake his hand. "What's up, my nigga?"

"Not shit, just chilling," Manus said solemnly.

"I've been trying to hit you, but I lost my phone."

"Rome told me."

"Have a seat."

Manus sat down and tried to relax some. His heart was racing. Noticing the pillows on the couch, he wondered whether they would really muffle a gunshot like on TV. He said, "I see you reading a good book."

"Yeah, it's off the chain, too. You read it before?"

"Yeah, when I was down."

"I feel that nigga Jay. Kind of reminds me of myself."

"How far you got?"

"I'm at the part where Tony and Jay got that broad Adrian trapped off in the truck and Jay wants to plug her."

"Oh yeah, shit about to get crazy now. I read that shit in one day."

"I heard about this shit happening for real, but the front of the book says it's fiction."

Manus shrugged.

L continued. "The dude that wrote the book, who the fuck is he? A college student trying to milk their story?"

"Nah, that nigga from around here. He street."

"Word? I ain't never heard of him."

"I don't know him personally, but him and my cousin Short is tight."

"You talking about Short from the Bricks?"

"Yeah."

"Yeah, I know him. He's shell." L then put the book down. "Oh, good look, too. Dude would've split my shit if it wasn't for you."

"It was nothing. I know you would've done the same for me."

"No doubt."

"I'm sorry about your boy. Have y'all found that nigga yet?"

"Hell nah. But I'll see him, though. That's my word."

"Oh yeah. I know what I meant to ask you," Manus said casually.

"What's that?"

"When the police had y'all hemmed up in the lobby, I heard dude say something about a Brad. Was he talking about the Brad that just got killed?"

"Uh, why you asked that?"

"'Cause that's my peoples and I want to know who killed him," Manus said, reaching.

*   *   *

Bobby watched his brother's casket get lowered into the ground. He had not attended Brian's wake or funeral because it was a sight that he could not bear. To him, it would be like looking at himself in the casket.

There were only twelve people at the burial site. Brian didn't have too many friends. They had long since been ran off by his funny and selfish ways. Lauren looked across at Brian's ex-wife, who was standing with a man that appeared to be in his late sixties. Lauren assumed that he was her father until he put his arm around her waist and kissed her on the mouth.

Not wanting to be there anymore, Lauren followed Bobby's lead as he walked away.

They were halfway to their cars when Bobby noticed that Lauren was behind him. "Oh, hey, Lauren."

"Hello, Bobby. You okay?"

"Yeah, I guess. I still can't believe he killed himself."

"Me either." Lauren leaned back on her car and stared at Bobby.

An awkward moment passed between them, and Bobby put his head down. The familiar feeling began to overwhelm him, so he reached in his pocket for his keys. "Well, I got to go. See you around."

As he turned to leave, Lauren said, "What have I ever done to you? Why do you hate me?"

Bobby stopped, but kept his back to her. "I don't hate you, Lauren. I never have."

"Then what is it, then?"

"It's too complicated." Then he started walking away.

"That's not fair, Bobby!"

Bobby spun around in a fury. "Don't tell me what's fair and what's not. I'm the one that got his soul mate snatched by his own bro —" Realizing what he said, he began to walk away again.

Lauren called him, but he ignored her. She caught up with him and grabbed his arm. "What are you talking about, Bobby?"

With the weight of Brian's death and the aura of Lauren's presence, Bobby began to cry. After all the years holding the secret in, he was sick of it. And before he knew it, he told her everything.

Lauren began to cry also.

"I'm so sorry, Lauren. I wanted to tell you, but I didn't want to ruin the family that y'all had."

"So it was you that I was with first?"

Bobby nodded.

Lauren began to cry harder. "You ... you never got the chance to know him. He needed you!"

Baffled, Bobby said, "Who?"

"Brad."

"Lauren, what are you saying?"

"You were my first, and I got pregnant the first time we were together."

*　　　*　　　*

L said, "Yeah, that's the same Brad. But I don't know who killed him."

"That nigga y'all was fighting … was that the same nigga that got hit with Brad?"

"I guess."

"Sounds like to me, Meat was insinuating that you had something to do with it. Why would he think that?"

L lit a cigarette. "'Cause he's fishing, that's why."

"I mean, something had to go on with y'all to make him think that. You got to tell me something!"

"Goddamn, dick! You acting like the police."

Manus stood up. "The police! Nigga, that was my muthafucking man that got killed. And anybody who I think had something to do with it, I'll ask them whatever. Fuck that!"

The tension in the room was thick. L stubbed out the half-smoked cigarette and lit another one. "Look, man, I was fucking with this broad that had dude gone. He was heated about it, but it wasn't that serious to me. All of this was going on during the same time dude got murked, so I guess that's why Meat is thinking I got something to do with it."

"So you fuck with that broad named Gloria?"

"Yeah. And I ain't speaking ill of the dead or nothing, but dude was bugging out over her. Trying to fight her in the club 'cause she wouldn't give him no play. That shit was so crazy."

Manus thought about the last conversation that he had had with Brad, and then replayed L's explanation in his mind. He knew it was a logical explanation and wasn't so sure that L had killed Brad now. He looked at the men and they seemed to be frozen with fear. Manus said, "Brad was like my brother. I'm just trying to find out what really happened to him."

"I feel exactly what you're saying," L said. "I'm in the exact same boat. It's crazy when your nigga is here one moment and gone the next."

After a moment, Manus sat back down and buried his face in his hands.

L and Rome looked at one another and sighed.

CHAPTER 17

Bobby stared at Lauren with his mouth agape.

Lauren said, "Are you okay?"

"He was my son?"

"Yes. I got pregnant the very first time."

Bobby's knees felt too weak, so he sat down on the ground. "I can't believe this."

Lauren, who was just as shocked about what he'd told her, sat down beside him. They sat in silence and observed the attention that they were attracting, but neither cared.

After a few minutes Bobby said, "This isn't fair! I don't know how I'm going to ever get over this."

Still crying, Lauren said, "We'll help each other get over it."

Bobby turned and looked at Lauren for a long moment. Then he got up and helped her up. "Lauren, please forgive me."

They embraced.

*   *   *

Manus pulled up at Erica's apartment complex and got out with a bag of toys that Grip had bought. He knocked lightly on the door.

"Who?" a man asked.

Oh shit! Manus thought. He knew that this moment would come sooner or later, but he still found himself caught off guard. Clearing his throat, he said, "It's Manus."

The door opened to reveal a chest-naked man with a pot gut. The men stared at one another for a moment.

Finally Manus said, "What's going on? You Charles?"

The man maintained his moody expression.

Gesturing at the bag, Manus said, "I just came —"

"He ain't here," the man said, cutting him off. "Ain't nobody here."

"I know. I just wanted to surprise him and Kandis."

"That's mine! Don't worry about Kandis."

Manus held up his hand. "Look, rap. I ain't trying to step on your toes with your daughter. I just didn't want to bring him something and leave her out. Feel me?" Charles stared at him coldly.

"Well, here you go, man," Manus said, setting the bag down. "I apologize if I disturbed you."

Charles grabbed the bag and slammed the door shut.

Manus got back in the car and headed home. He couldn't blame Charles for acting like that; he felt his pain.

When he arrived home, Grip was sitting in the den watching the Clippers play. "Unc, what's up?"

"Nothing much. Just watching my team dig in some ass."

"Yeah, they stepped it up this year."

"All we need is a few more Duke players and we'll be straight. Brand and Magette can't do it all by themselves."

"You right."

"You dropped them kids' toys off yet?"

"Yeah, I just did it."

"Sit down. Let me holla at you for a second."

Manus sat down. "What's up?"

"How you and your girlfriend doing?"

"We straight. She's finishing up her classes to be a dentist."

"Are you happy with her?"

"Yeah, Unc. She's good as gold."

"Then why are you walking around here like you lost your best friend?"

"'Cause I did."

"Oh. You still grieving over Brad."

"How can I not grieve? The nigga who saved my life is dead and don't nobody know who killed him. I just feel so messed up about the whole thing."

"I know the feeling, but there's nothing you can do to bring him back."

"I know. But if I could find out who killed him, I'll be able to rest better. I know his mom would."

"And if you was to find out who did it, what would you do?"

"Probably get even."

"Listen, Manus. I know that you feel like you owe Brad, but you got to stop and think. Ain't no telling what Brad got himself into. A person that's confined can be a totally different person on the streets."

"Brad was a good dude, though."

"And I don't doubt that. All I'm saying is ain't no telling what's surrounding the situation. Look, you're grown and I can't tell you what to do, but I'll be damned if I let you throw away your life. Especially in a situation where you don't know all the facts. When Leet died, I promised myself that I was going to raise and protect you like my own, and that's what I intend to do. That's my obligation. I done let you talk me into this drug shit, and now you want to play gangster? Nah, that ain't gonna work. Either you gonna get money, or you gonna be a gangster. You can't do both. Conflict won't allow it. Now, I need to know right now what you gonna do, 'cause I'll call Six and end y'all relationship."

After a moment of pondering, Manus said, "I'mma get money."

"You sure?"

"Yeah."

"I ain't playing now."

"Me either. I'm for real."

Grip was silent for a minute. He stared at Manus. He had never known him to be a liar. "Speaking of Six, how's everything going with y'all?"

"Not good. I don't know what's going on. I haven't heard from him in a week and a half, and I'm almost on *E*."

"Let me tell you something about this game, because I've been noticing something you're doing. I understand that you just got out and you want to catch up on the things that you haven't done. But your spending habits are worse than mine. Getting fast money doesn't mean you have to spend it fast. A lot of hustlers that work for someone make the mistake of spending their money instead of stacking it so they can become their own boss. Once you accomplish that, then you can make whatever moves you choose. Six hasn't forgotten about you. He's his own boss, and he moves according to how he feels."

*   *   *

Meat walked in Kerr Drugs and went to the cold medicine aisle. His head throbbed like it was about to split. He found what he was looking for and went to the cash register to pay for it.

On his way out, he was so caught up in his thoughts that he bumped into a woman. "Oh, I'm sorry. I ... *Tip*. What's going on?"

"Nothing," she said, as she continued to go her way.

"Tip, what's up? I know you ain't still mad at me. It wasn't that serious."

Tip continued walking.

For some reason, Meat felt obligated to settle their differences. He took off after her. When he caught up with her, he said, "Tip, why you tripping on me like that? I ain't know you took that shit to heart like that. My bad."

"Why apologize for being the way you are?"

"'Cause my way ain't always right, that's why." Meat held out his hand. "Please accept my apology."

Tip looked at his hand, and then his face. To her, he seemed sincere. And plus, she couldn't help but notice how fine he still was. She took his hand. "You flipped on me, Meat. I thought we were better than that."

"My bad, Tip. I be on some other shit at times."

"I couldn't believe how greasy you handled me. I know I wasn't your girl or nothing, but I needed you. Look at what we had just went through. Lost our best friends, and almost died ourselves, and all you cared about was a nut." Tip's eyes spilled over with tears and Meat wiped them away with his thumbs.

"Don't cry. What are you about to do?"

Tip sniffled. "Get my granddaddy a birthday card."

"And after that?"

"Nothing."

"Can we go somewhere and talk?"

Tip looked at him suspiciously.

Meat said, "Just to talk. At a restaurant or somewhere."

"I guess. Just to talk, right?"

"That's all."

"Okay, let me get this card first."

Meat left his car in the plaza's parking lot and rode with Tip.

She said, "Let's just ride around. I'm really not hungry."

Meat popped the cold tablets. "Me either."

"You sick?"

"Not really. Just a light head cold."

"Oh."

They rode in silence. Then out of the blue Tip said, "I can't seem to get that night off my mind. I'm starting to remember a lot of things that didn't seem relevant then."

"Yeah? Like what?"

"A lot of things. And then I heard about your incident at the show."

"Yeah, that was some bullshit."

She looked at him. "Did you do it?"

"Do what?"

"Kill Tee?"

"Even if I didn't, I got the credit for it."

"He deserved it."

"Why you say that?"

"Like I said, a lot of things came back to me that didn't seem relevant then."

"But you still ain't saying nothing."

"I remember seeing L and them at the club that night. I remember seeing Brad watching that girl, Gloria, that I found out later was his ex. And on top of that, I seen L and two other guys not too long ago. When L seen me, he gave me this funny look. Right then I knew. He confirmed my suspicions."

"Of what?"

"That he was the one that shot us, or had something to do with it." Tears began to flow from Tip's eyes again.

Meat said, "Who was the guys that was with L?"

"Rome and a guy named Manus."

"Manus? I heard that name somewhere before. Manus? Manus? Was he a tall, brown-skinned guy with corn rows?"

"Uhm-hmm."

"I seen him with L and them the night we got to fighting, but I ain't know who he was."

Meat rubbed his chin. "I heard that name somewhere before."

"Do you know an old coon named Grip?"

"That owns that detail shop on Chapel Hill Street?"

"Yeah."

"I don't know him personally, but I know who you're talking about. What about him?"

"Well, that's his uncle. He just got out not too long ago."

"Who, Manus?"

"Yep."

"Oh my muthafucking God!"

"What?" Tip asked, startled.

"That's the Manus that Brad used to talk about all the time. I'mma kill that nigga!"

Tip was surprised by Meat's comment. "What has happened to you, Meat? You're not a thug. Please don't let all this stuff change you."

"I'm not. I'll always be me. It's just that my man looked up to that nigga, and come to find out he's fucking with the niggas that killed him."

"Maybe he doesn't know."

"That nigga know. That's how the fight started at the club. I bet that nigga had Brad killed."

"So what are you going to do, throw away your life?"

"Nah, but what security do I have knowing that the same niggas that killed my man, and almost killed us, is still walking around? At any given time, they might decide that they're not comfortable with me still alive and come to finish me."

"Listen, Meat. You don't even have to worry about none of that stuff. I got some money from selling my shop, and you could just leave with me. We could start over somewhere."

"I'm not the type to run away from situations."

"You ain't running; you're just being smart. The way things are going now, you're either going to be locked up or dead."

"So now you're bad mouthing me?"

"No, Meat! I don't want none of that to happen to you. That's why I'm asking you to leave with me. Please."

Meat thought about that for a moment. "I appreciate it, Tip, but I can't. I'mma give them niggas what they want."

BOOK II – DEATH

I've been low; I've been high, both chemically and mentally –
I've done things that, now, don't even make sense to me.
I've been loved; I've been hated; but mostly I've been hurt –
And it shaded my character to the point of committing and
expecting dirt.
I've been saved; I've been an atheist, all in my search of self –
Through living I've learned that the only thing for certain is death.

From the book of Flagrant Sorrows
By: Kevin Bullock

CHAPTER 18

Manus stood in the line at Italian Pizzeria trying to remember exactly what Gee wanted on her chicken parmesan sub. He noticed a man that was sitting in a booth staring at him.

"May I help you?" the chubby Italian asked from behind the counter.

Manus stepped up to the counter. "Let me get a chicken parmesan sub with only lettuce and tomatoes, one steak and cheese sub with only lettuce and mayo, and two slices of cheese pizza."

"Do you want anything to drink with that?"

"Yeah. Give me two lemonades."

"What size?"

"Medium."

The Italian rung the order up. "That'll be $15.02."

After Manus paid the man, the Italian said, "Is that to go?"

"Yeah." Manus sat down at the nearest vacant booth to wait. Once again, he noticed the man in a different booth still staring at him. Tired of it, Manus acknowledged the man with a nod.

The man nodded back.

Manus felt fatigued from not getting enough sleep lately. He also knew that fifty percent of it was mental stress. He had always known and admired Pat for his mental strength. Pat had served ten years of a life sentence, but instead of going crazy, as Manus believed he would, Pat had always kept hope alive. But in their last conversation, Pat was clearly teetering on the brink of going off. Manus wanted nothing more than to help him, but right now he needed help for himself. Things were crazy.

Manus was a long way from his goal. Over the past week he'd resorted to selling dimes of crack, and had barely made a decent profit. Petty hand-to-hand transactions was still beneath him, but being broke wasn't an option. Manus opened his eyes when he felt someone tap him on the shoulder.

"Excuse me," the man that had been staring at him said.

Frowning, Manus sat up straight. "What's up?"

"My bad for disturbing you, but you look so familiar. Do I know you?"

Manus studied the man's face. "Not that I know of."

"Are you sure? Because I never forget a face."

"I'm positive," Manus said, getting irritated.

"I know you from somewhere. Hold up, it's going to come to me." The man put his fist to his head and appeared to be in deep thought. Manus opened his mouth to tell the man to get away from him but the man spoke first.

"I got it! You're Six's peoples, right?"

"Uh ... yeah," Manus said hesitantly.

The man got excited. "I knew I knew you from somewhere. That's why I kept staring at you. You don't remember me?"

Manus studied the man's face once again but didn't recognize him. "Nah, where do I suppose to know you from?"

The man sat across from Manus then whispered, "I was over Moe's house when you whipped them thangs up for him. Remember, I was the one that got bit on the calf by that crazy-ass chow?"

"Yeah," Manus said, now remembering the crazed chow that had chased the stranger when he got out of his car. "I remember you now. You cut your hair, didn't you?"

"Yeah, I had to switch my appearance."

"What's up with Moe?"

"Moe caught three years about two weeks ago."

"Yeah? That's fucked up."

"Yeah, it is. It's been real crazy since he's been gone. I've been trying to hold the fort down, but I can't seem to find shit. Where's Six at? He haven't been answering his phone."

"That's a good fucking question."

"What's your name again?"

"Manus."

The man extended his hand. "Mark." They shook hands and Mark whispered, "I know that you're still doing your thing."

"A lil' something."

"Look, my money is low. I need you to sell me like nine of them things.

"Whole ones?"

"Nah. Onions. I'll shoot you seven thousand."

Manus' mind began pacing. He knew he could buy an eighth of a kilo and whip it to nine ounces easily.

Mark mistook Manus' hesitation for paranoia and said, "Come on, baby. Do that for me. I'm good peoples."

Playing it off, Manus said, "I don't know, man. I really don't like to deal outside of my circle, you know?"

"I understand, but it's all gravy with me. I'm just trying to flip my dough before I go broke. You know how it be when you can't find shit but you're steadily spending money. I've been doing that shit for two weeks now and I done went from a whole one, to what I'm trying to get from you."

Manus let about five seconds pass before saying, "Give me your number, and I'll get back with you."

"Thank you, man. I really appreciate it."

"It's gravy."

As soon as Mark gave him the number, he said, "You know I need that in powder, right?"

Damn! Manus thought. Then he said, "Yeah, I know."

"No disrespect or anything, but I seen your whip game first hand."

"It's gravy."

As soon as Mark left the restaurant, Manus dialed his connect's number.

"Hello? First Baptist Church."

"This Manus. What's good?"

"Who did you say this was?"

"Manus."

"Who do you want to speak to? Everybody has already left out of the church."

Realizing what was going on, Manus said, "I'm the one that Wheat has been bringing over there."

"Oh, oh. What's up, my nigga? My fault. I be 'noid."

"I feel you."

"What's good, though?"

"I'm trying to see if everything's everything."

"Oh, you must be a pain freak. I beat you five times straight on *Live*. Come over here in two hours and I'll let you pick an All-star team. I'll beat you with '05' Lakers."

Reading between the lines, Manus said, "We'll see when I get there."

"Two hours."

"I'll be there."

*　　　*　　　*

Gee balled up the aluminum foil. "That was good, baby. Thank you."

"You're welcome." Manus put his foil paper from the sub in the bag and was about to stand.

Gee said, "I got it. Relax."

After she threw the trash in the garbage can, she said, "You want some ice cream? I got cookies and cream."

"Nah, I'm straight. I got to go."

"Where are you about to go?"

Gee's question caught him completely off guard. It wasn't her style to question him about where he went or had been. Manus recollected himself and said, "I got to go handle some business. Why? What's up?"

"I don't know, baby. That question just came out of nowhere."

He studied her face. "Are you okay?"

"I was. For some reason, I all of a sudden started feeling queasy."

"It might be from the food. Go lie down for a minute; it'll pass."

"I wish you could lay with me."

Manus looked at his watch and saw that he only had forty-five minutes before it was time to meet his connect. "I wish I could, too, but I really have to make this run."

"Okay."

"You okay?"

"I will be."

Manus kissed her and headed toward the door.

"Manus."

He turned around. "Huh?"

"Call me when you're done, okay?"

"Okay."

*   *   *

Manus pulled up at the house located in North Durham. Two identical twins around age seven, stood in the yard playing catch with a tennis ball and mitt.

When Manus got out of his car, the twins stopped playing and watched him.

"What's up lil' twins?"

"Our names ain't no *twins*."

"My bad. What's y'all names?"

"I'm Derrick."

"And I'm Darrick."

"Well, what's up Derrick and Darrick?"

Simultaneously, the twins said, "What's up?"

Derrick said, "You come to see my daddy or my momma?"

"I come to see your daddy."

Derrick whispered something in his brother's ear.

Darrick said, "My daddy's friends spend more than my momma's friends, so you have to give us ten dollars apiece to get what you need from our daddy." Both boys blocked Manus' path.

Just then, a house window opened and Manus' connect, Black, stuck his head out the window. "I heard y'all this time! I'mma beat y'all ass; come on in here!"

The twins looked at one another and took off running down the street.

"Get y'all bad asses back here!" Black disappeared from the window and appeared at the front door. He watched his sons turn the corner. Then he looked at Manus. "I swear, them some bad-ass kids. I knew they were up to something when their momma found three hundred dollars in their room."

Manus laughed. "They're starting early, ain't they?"

Black nodded his head in despair. "That's all they see. I'm doing my thing; their mother," he said, pointing inside the house, "is doing her thing, so I don't know why I'm surprised."

Manus knew all too well about inheriting ways from parents.

"Come on in."

Manus trailed Black through the house and saw a woman sitting at a table that was completely covered with marijuana.

Black stopped and said to the woman, "I caught your bad-ass kids trying to swindle my man out of some money."

The woman frowned. "Where they ass at now? I need to beat their asses."

"They made a left on Belvin, wide open."

"They'll be back when they get hungry, and I'm tearing their asses up when they do."

Black said, "Oh, this is Manus. Manus, this is my wife, Toya."

Manus said, "How you doing?"

"Fine, and you?"

"I'm good."

"Come on," Black said, leaving the room.

Black led him in a den and shut the door.

"What are you trying to get?"

"I'm trying to cop."

"Seven grams?"

"Nah, nine ounces."

"Damn! You been grinding."

"Hell yeah."

Black went to the closet and came back with a book bag. He began to pull ounces out and said, "How much you got?"

"I got five."

Black stopped pulling out the ounces. "Man, I can't give you nine for that much. I wouldn't really be making shit. But I tell you what. Since you're Wheat's boy, I'll give it to you for sixty-five."

"All I got is five right now. Let me owe you the fifteen; I'm good for it."

Shaking his head, Black said, "I don't hustle like that. I'm strictly C.O.D."

Manus sighed. He was distraught.

Black saw the frustration in Manus' face and said, "Okay, okay. This is the best I can do: Give me the five, and I'll give you eight of them. You can't beat that."

Manus was about to call the whole thing off, but when he thought about the container of acetone that he had at home, he came up with an idea.

"Yeah, you're right. Let me get it."

CHAPTER 19

"**W**ho is it?" a woman asked in Spanish.

"It's Amado."

The door opened and a woman in her late forties stood in the doorway.

"Amado. How have you been?"

Amado embraced José's widow, Fransica, and said, "Good. What about you?"

"I'm okay."

"What about the kids?"

"Celia made the honor roll, and Rigo is still struggling with his father's death."

A lump formed in Amado's throat. "We all are."

Fransica's eyes began to get misty. She blinked the tears back and said, "Come on in; let me fix you something to eat. It looks like you haven't eaten in weeks."

Following her to the kitchen, Amado realized that, since José's death, he had mostly drank coffee and enough food to ease the hunger pain away.

As Fransica fixed Amado's plate, he sat down at the table in a daze. It had taken everything that he had just to make this visit, but out of respect and loyalty, Amado knew he had to check on José's family.

Fransica broke his daze. "How is your kids and wife?"

"They have everything they need, so I guess they're okay. What about you?"

"Things have been so different for me lately. Yes, nothing has been the same since José has been gone. I don't have anyone to argue with anymore. I miss him so much that I light his cigars at night when I go to bed. The familiar fragrance gives my heart temporary security that he's still with me."

Amado was quiet for a moment, then he said, "You know I'm going to avenge José's death, right?"

Still at the stove, Fransica put her head down and began to shiver.

Amado continued, "Maybe our pains will ease up after that?"

In a voice barely audible, Fransica said, "Why didn't you go with him?"

"I didn't know anything about it. He made me take a couple of days off."

As if she didn't hear him, Fransica said, "It was your responsibility to protect him and you failed!"

Fransica's words hit Amado like a Mack truck. The lump in his throat throbbed so hard that Amado found it difficult to breath. "Fransica, as God as my witness, José' forced me to take those days off! I only agreed when he promised that he wouldn't conduct any business on those days."

Fransica just stood there, still shivering.

Amado got up to console her.

She sensed him coming. "Don't!" she screamed. "I don't care if he *fired* you. You knew just as I did that Gonzalez was a fool."

Amado froze in his tracks.

She continued, "I don't blame you entirely for José's death, because he should have seen through Gonzalez also. But as much as he has done for you and your family, it would seem like to me that the actual killers should have been long dead by now."

"But —"

"No buts!" she screamed. "There's no excuse."

Amado knew that she was right, so he didn't bother to defend himself anymore. Everything that she was telling him, he had already told himself.

Fransica faced him and said, "I love you and your family. We have all been very close over the years, but I cannot continue our friendship anymore until those people are taken care of."

She then sat the plate of chili con carne on the table. "Hurry and eat so you can leave."

*   *   *

"Hello?"

"Can I speak to Mark?"

"This is him. Who is this?"

"This is Manus."

"What's up, my man? Tell me something good."

"Meet me at the same place in thirty."

"Look, my wife just left with my car, so we got to meet near my house somewhere."

"That's cool. Where do you want to meet?"

"Uh, let me see. Oh yeah, do you know where Alma Street is at?"

"Nah, I ain't never heard of that street."

"What about that store on the corner of Holloway and Guthrie Street?"

"Do it got a pool hall on one side of it?"

"Yeah, that's it."

"Yeah, I know where it's at. That's where you want to meet at?"

"Yeah, how soon can you get there?"

"About twenty minutes."

"Word. I'll be standing at the pay phones."

"A'ight." Manus ended the call and proceeded with his plan. After he added an ounce of acetone with the cocaine to make it a quarter kilo, he crushed some of the solid powder up so that it would blend in with the cutting agent. Although he would only make two thousand off the deal if it went through, it was an easy two thousand. And that was the best money to him. Easy.

Manus had decided that the profit he would make off Mark would be used to buy a quarter kilo. And with his whip game, he knew that there was no turning back.

*   *   *

Gee flipped through the TV stations trying to find something to watch that would occupy her mind. She couldn't explain it, but she knew that something wasn't right. First came the queasiness, and now she was having an anxiety attack. No matter how much she tried to think otherwise, Gee knew that all of this had something to do with Manus.

She admitted to herself that ever since he had told her about his illegal occupation, her nerves had been wrecked. Every time he left her, she prayed silently that this wouldn't be her last time seeing him alive.

But today was different. She had automatically went in panic mode when he had said he was about to leave. Gee reached for the phone but jerked back. She didn't want Manus to think she had become obsessive. The look on his face, when she had asked him where he was going, told her that he didn't enjoy being questioned.

Gee sat there and watched old episodes of Martin. Her mind was completely off Manus until Martin chased Gina into the bedroom with sex in his eyes. Anxiety began to set in and Gee decided that she would rather have an irritated boyfriend than a dead one.

She picked up the phone and called her man.

*   *   *

As soon as Manus pulled into the store's parking lot, he immediately spotted Mark talking on one of the pay phones.

Mark spotted the Camry and hung up the phone.

Manus pulled up beside him and Mark got in.

"What's the deal?" he asked as he shut the door.

"Chillin', chillin'. What's —" Manus' phone began to ring. Manus looked at the display and saw the word *Wifey*.

He turned to Mark. "Hold up." Then he answered the phone. "What's up, baby?"

Gee said, "Please don't be mad at me, but I just called to see if you were okay."

"I'm not mad. And, yes, everything's cool."

"I have a crazy feeling. Can you please come back here after you finish doing what you're doing?"

"Yeah, I can do that."

"Thank you."

"It's nothing. Are you okay now?"

"Yes. I love you."

"I love you, too."

Manus ended the call and turned back to Mark. "My bad, man."

"Don't apologize; I do the same thing. It's nothing like having someone; I've been married for six years."

"Yeah?"

"The best six years of my life."

Manus thought about that and then got down to business. "You wanted a quarter, right?"

"Yeah."

Manus reached under his seat and grabbed a lunch box. Keeping it below window level, he handed it to Mark.

Mark sat the lunch box on the floor between his feet and opened it. Then he pulled the bag out and examined the coke.

"It's a lot of shake in it, isn't it?"

"A lil' bit, but it's all good, though."

Mark examined the coke for a few seconds longer before putting it back in the lunch box. "It'll work. Don't nobody else around here got nothing, so it's going to sell, regardless of what."

"I didn't touch it," Manus said, defending himself.

"Oh, I ain't say you did. I'm just saying that even if I had some numbing powder it'll sell, because ain't nothing around here."

"Oh."

Mark reached on the inside of his jacket and pulled out a brown bag. He opened it and pulled out a stack of money. "These are all thousand stacks," he said, handing him the stack. "You can count it but you got to be careful with Mr. Smith's nosey ass because he'll call the police." Mark handed him the brown bag.

Manus looked in the bag and saw six more stacks.

As he began to count the first stack, Mark said, "look at this nosey muthafucka."

Manus looked at the store's window and saw an older man staring at them.

Mark said, "I'll call you probably tomorrow for another one. I know that this is about to go fast. You going to have it, right?"

Manus put the stack back in the bag and said, "Yeah, just call me."

"A'ight then, be careful."

"You too."

The men shook hands and Mark got out of the car with the lunchbox in the inside of his jacket.

Manus pulled out of the parking lot and dialed Black's number.

"Hello? First Baptist Church."

"What's up? This Manus again."

"What's up, my nigga?"

"Are you trying to see me in *Live*? I got this memory card with a code that let's us get all of the best players that ever played on that team."

"Damn, my nigga. You're about fifteen minutes too late."

"Yeah?"

"Yeah, man, my bad-ass sons are playing on it and it might be three hours before they get off it."

"Well I'll call you back then."

"A'ight."

Manus ended the call and headed back to Gee's house. He felt satisfied with the quick take. Once Black restocked his supplies, Manus would buy the quarter kilo and whip it to a half kilo. After that he would hustle on Dawkins with half grams for fifteen dollars. Manus knew that no crackhead or hustler could resist such prices, even when the drug has been cut. It was a quick come up.

He then thought about Gee and the way that she had been acting lately. He suspected that it was over him telling her that he hustled. Whatever it was, Manus knew that he had to talk to her without giving her the impression that he was aggravated.

When he arrived at her house, she met him at the door and hugged him.

Manus kissed her forehead, "Baby, what's wrong?"

"I don't know. I'm just feeling strange for some reason."

Closing the door behind him, Manus said, "It wouldn't have anything to do with what I do, would it?"

"Uh..."

"Be honest."

"I am. To tell you the truth, it has everything to do with it. I'm just scared that I'm going to lose you."

Manus hugged her again. "You're not going to lose me."

"I hope not. I already don't really have anyone. My mother is dead, and me and my father's relationship is strained."

"Baby, I promise you I'm not going anywhere. At least not for the next fifty years."

Gee stood on her tip toes and began to kiss him.

As he kissed her, he picked her up and carried her to the bedroom. Once they were out of their clothes, Manus realized he didn't have a condom.

Breathing hard, Gee said, "What? Why you stop?"

"I don't have a condom."

Gee pondered on it a moment before helping Manus to get on top of her.

*   *   *

An hour later, Manus and Gee lay in the bed naked. Gee said, "I can stay like this forever."

"Yeah?"

"Uhm-hmm."

"What would we do for money?"

Gee playfully punched him in the side. "Smart butt."

Manus laughed.

Gee looked on the floor and saw the brown bag. "What's in the bag, food?"

"Oh," Manus said, getting out of the bed. "I got to count this right quick."

"I'll help."

Manus dumped the money out on the bed and began to count the stack that he had started on in the car.

Gee grabbed another stack and began to count it. "It's sure a lot of ones here."

Manus looked up from his stack and saw all of the one-dollar bills that Gee was counting. "Hold up!" he said, grabbing another stack.

He pulled the rubber band off the stack and saw all of the one-dollar bills beneath a twenty.

"Fuck!" He checked the rest of the stacks and saw that they were the same way.

"What, baby?" Gee asked.

Manus retrieved his phone and dialed Mark's number. He didn't get an answer. After the third try, Manus set the phone down and lay back on the bed.

"What's wrong, baby?"

"I got got."

Gee frowned. "Got got?"

Manus sighed. "Yeah, the dude tricked me into believing that he was giving me seven thousand dollars."

"And you gave him your stuff?"

Manus nodded.

Gee remembered that he had told her that he didn't deal the drugs, but she knew that this wasn't the time to bring it up. So she only said, "I'm sorry."

Manus nodded and closed his eyes in frustration. He felt like a fool for falling for the oldest trick in the book. Manus knew that this was definitely something that he would take to the grave with him.

Chapter 20

In Honey's restaurant, Meat and Tasha looked through a baby dictionary while waiting for their food.

Tasha said, "What about Santraile?"

"Hell nah. That sounds almost like a broad's name. My son got to have a fly name."

"Let's just make him a junior then?"

"Nah. I don't really like my first name like that. It's too plain."

"Demetrius is a cute name."

"Yeah, right. You're just saying that."

"Why you always think I only say things that you want to hear? Have you ever thought that maybe we're just on the same page?"

"Yeah, but still. I think that you sometimes just be trying to please me."

"If I wanted to please you, I'll do something like this." Tasha slid her foot out of her slides and found Meat's crotch. She ran her toes lightly over it and felt him grow.

"A'ight, girl. We going to jail for indecent exposure."

Tasha got up and sat beside Meat. Her hand was lowered under the table to undo his zipper.

"Girl! You better stop," he said, laughing.

He grabbed her hand and said, "Let's go! You got me all fucked up."

"Where we going? We're waiting on our food."

"Man, fuck that food. We'll order a pizza."

For the first time, Tasha saw urgency in Meat's eyes. She had never seen him eager to do anything. And the fact that it was she whom he was eager for made Tasha just as eager for him. She said, "My apartment is closer."

"I can't wait that long. The Red Roof is right across the lot."

Tasha grabbed his hand. "Let's go!"

*   *   *

When Manus stepped in Devine's Sports Bar, his cell phone began to ring. "Hello?"

"I'mma kill your ass, bitch!"

"Who the fuck is this?"

"Don't worry about all that. You just better hope you got your ratchet on you, 'cause it's going down as soon as you come back out."

"Nigga, fuck —" Manus stopped talking when he saw L and Rome in the corner of the bar laughing. L had his cell phone in his hand. Manus ended the call and went over to them. "You fucked me up on that one."

After L and Rome's laughter subsided, L said, "Yeah, nigga, I got your ass. You was hyped." The men shook hands.

Manus said, "I haven't heard from y'all in a minute."

"That's 'cause we ain't had shit. I don't know what's up with Six. Dick won't take my calls or nothing."

"You too? I'm freelancing like crazy, trying to make ends meet. I even found myself pitching dimes on Dawkins."

"Dawkins! That hot-ass street, you going to jail."

"I'm desperate. Six left a nigga hanging."

"I feel you. A nigga got to do what he got to do."

"Hell yeah," Rome said.

"But I don't know what's up with Six. I think them boys are watching him."

"For real?"

"I'm guessing. But whatever it is, it got me thirty-eight hot. Dude ain't letting a nigga know shit, like fuck me or something," L said.

Manus observed the men in their new clothes and gleaming jewelry. "Y'all niggas don't look like y'all are hurting too much to me."

Rome said, "You always got to keep more than one hustle."

Manus started to ask what their other hustle was, but instead he said, "Maybe I should be rolling with y'all niggas then, greasy as I am."

L and Rome looked at each other. L then pulled out some money.

"You're a cool-ass nigga. I like your style. You might not want to take this from me, but I'll be insulted if you didn't." L counted out a thousand dollars and handed it to Manus. "Don't look at this as a handout. Look at it as pay in advance."

Manus was speechless.

*　　　*　　　*

Now that Six had unofficially retired, he had more free time on his hands than he knew what to do with. For the first month, he enjoyed lying around the house doing nothing all day. But eventually he became restless. Almost claustrophobic. That's when he came up with an idea, picked up the phone, and called Grip.

"Hello? Grip asked.

"What's up, partner?"

"You must be telepathic, 'cause I was just about to call you."

"What's up?"

"I don't want to sound like I'm meddling, but I wanted to ask you about my nephew and you."

"Look, hold that thought. What are you doing for the next few days?"

"I don't have anything planned. What's up?"

"What do you say to that long-overdue fishing trip that we been putting off for years?"

"Sounds good to me. When you trying to leave?"

"Sheeit, I'm leaving out the door now."

Grip laughed. "Nah. I got to take care of a few things first. But we can leave first thing in the morning."

"I'm packing now."

*　　　*　　　*

Grip dialed his friend Frena's number.

"Hello?"

"Hello, sweetheart."

"Hello yourself."

"I know that tone. What's wrong?"

"That same female that came over here looking for you ...

keyed my car."

"What! When?"

"I guess she did it last night because it wasn't like that yesterday."

"I'm sorry, baby. I'll pay to get your car repainted."

"Don't worry about it; my insurance will pay for it. I'm just tired of that … ooh! I'm not even going to stoop to her level."

"Calm down, baby."

"No. You just tell that girl that she's going to jail the next time she pulls something crazy like that."

"Baby, honestly, I don't talk to that girl. Nor do I know how to get in touch with her. She's just a crazy-ass female that's trying to get a free ride."

"Grip, I told you when we first got together that I didn't care about your other women as long as I didn't see them."

"Baby, listen to me. I give you my word that I don't mess with that woman in any sort of fashion. I haven't brought any problems in this relationship, and that's how I intend to keep it."

Five seconds passed before Frena said, "Well you better get a restraining order on her or something, because she's getting bolder and bolder by the day. Soon she might try to break in the house to trash it."

"Nah, it's not going that far. Whenever I run into her again, I'll put a cease to all of it. Okay?"

"Okay."

"Not trying to change the subject or anything, but I need a favor from you."

"What, baby?"

"I need for you to go down to the laundromat in Wellons Village at nine o'clock and let the repairman in. I'm going to be out of town for a few days."

"Okay, no problem."

"Thanks."

"Can you come see me tonight? It's been a week."

"Uh, yeah. You got to come and get me, though. Because if that girl key any one of my babies, I might kill her."

*   *   *

"Who is it?" Meat asked.

"Domino's Pizza," a man yelled back.

Meat opened the door of the hotel room half way, shielding his mostly naked body. A fat black man who was sweating profusely said, "How are you doing, sir? Did you order a pizza?"

"Yeah."

"Okay. I got a large barbecue chicken pizza with extra cheese for you. That'll be thirteen forty-five."

Meat looked at Tasha, who was in the bed. "Baby, throw me my pants right there on the floor."

Tasha sat up and the sheet fell from her bare breasts.

After he caught the pants and retrieved the money, he turned around and saw the pizza man looking past him. "Goddamn, don't break your neck."

The pizza man peeled his eyes off Tasha. "Oh, my fault, sir. I didn't mean no disrespect."

"It's gravy," Meat said, handing him fifteen dollars.

The pizza man reached in his pocket to get Meat's change.

Meat said, "Go 'head. Keep it."

"Thank you. Enjoy."

Meat closed the door but quickly reopened it and stuck his head out. "Hey!"

The pizza man turned around. "Yes?"

"Where's my waters at?"

"I ain't know nothing about any waters. They weren't on your bill."

"Goddamn. A'ight, man."

Meat slammed the door and set the pizza on the table.

Tasha saw him getting dressed and said, "Where you about to go?"

"To the vending machine. What kind of juice you want?"

"I want a grape soda."

"You ain't gonna keep feeding my baby all that acid. Now, what kind of juice you want?"

"Apple."

Meat kissed her. "Thank you."

He left the room but came right back in and went to the nightstand. He opened the drawer and grabbed the .38 Special from beside the Bible. He was out the door again.

Meat pressed the elevator button and waited. When the doors opened, Meat looked up and hesitated. After that, everything seemed to happen in slow motion. He was staring into the faces of L and Rome.

All three men froze in place, shocked to see each other.

Meat quickly got over his shock and began walking backwards. He fumbled for his gun and finally fired three shots at the men. He heard someone yell as he took off toward the stairs. Without thinking, Meat jumped down the whole first flight of stairs. He landed wrong and fell hard. The gun came out of his hand and slid two feet away. He got up and retrieved it.

L appeared at the top of the stairs and began firing at him.

Meat dove halfway down the second flight of stairs and rolled down the rest. He jumped to his feet and let off his last two shots at L, who was now at the top of the second flight.

L retreated.

Meat hobbled to the first floor. As he struggled toward his car, he reached in his pocket for his keys. He pressed a remote auto-start button and jumped into his car. Meat sped out of the parking lot and into the oncoming traffic with nothing but a sprained ankle.

*　　　*　　　*

"Answer something for me, Grip," Manus said.

"What's that?"

"Why my momma kill Big Leet?"

"Uh, I guess she did it in a rage."

"No. I mean, for what reason?"

Grip let some time pass before saying, "'Cause she found out he had another woman pregnant."

"What? So that means I got a sibling running around somewhere?"

"I don't know. The woman left town after Leet was killed and ain't nobody heard from her since."

Manus walked to the window and stared out. "She still ain't have to kill him, though."

"Look, Manus. I'm not trying to justify what she done, but Leet took your mother through some shit. When she had you she had some complications, and the doctor told her that she couldn't have any more babies. She was crushed because she knew that Leet wanted a big family. I guess she couldn't handle the fact that Leet was making a family with someone else."

"That was a selfish move."

"I agree. But don't never think for one moment that she ain't love you. She loves you more than life itself."

Manus thought about that for a moment, but the pain from missing his father clouded reason. He got off the subject before he could get depressed. "So, where y'all gonna fish at? Off the pier?"

"Nah, off the boat. We're going for the gusto."

"Word."

Grip sensed that Manus wanted to say something else. "What is it? What's on your mind?"

"What's up with Six?"

"I'll find out on the trip."

"Nah, I'm talking about what's *really* up with him?"

"What do you mean?"

"Is the feds watching him?"

"Not that I know of. What made you ask that?"

"Well, you know I be dealing with his man named L now."

"The one that was fighting at the club?"

"Yeah. Anyway, he told me that Six just cut him back for no reason, too. He guessed that the feds was watching Six and making him lay low."

"I don't know. Have L been coming up short with Six's money or something?"

"I doubt it. That nigga is a money magnet."

Grip stroked his chin. He didn't think Six would drag him in on a conspiracy. Six was one of the most honorable guys that he knew. But in all the years of knowing Six, he had never known him to turn down the opportunity to make money. And now that he thought about it, something was definitely wrong. Grip said, "I don't know about that one, but I'll find out."

*　　　*　　　*

The ringing of the phone woke Charles. "Hello?"

"Let me speak to Erica," Shawnda said.

Charles looked at the clock. "Do you have any goddamn respect for anybody else in this house? Shawnda, it's fucking one-thirty in the goddamn morning!"

Erica heard the commotion and rolled over to Charles. "Give me the phone, Charles."

Charles handed it to her. "You better tell her something. That shit don't make no goddamn sense, waking up everybody and shit!"

"You the one that's waking everybody up. Go back to sleep."

"I hate that bitch!" Charles said as he rolled over.

"Hello?"

"Bitch, he tripping, ain't he?"

"As usual. What's up, girl?"

"Guess who just got killed?"

"Who, girl?"

"Black ass Rome. The one I used to mess with."

"For real! Who killed him, girl?"

"Pretty boy Meat."

"Damn, girl! He knocking them niggas off."

"Yeah, bitch. They say he caught his baby's momma getting off the elevator with Rome."

"For real! Who's his baby's momma?"

"I don't know, but whoever she is she must be nice with hers 'cause Meat don't care nothing about a bitch."

"Damn, girl. Durham is getting crazier and crazier."

"I know. I can't wait 'til the wake and funeral. You know it's gonna be plenty of ballers there."

"You know it is."

"You going with me in the morning to find something to wear there?"

"Yeah, I'll go."

"A'ight then, bitch."

"Bye."

CHAPTER 21

At noon the next day, Lauren stood before the mirror, naked, and examined her body. Other than her six pack, she basically had the same body she'd had when she was eighteen.

She went to her dresser and pulled open the drawer that she kept her panties and bras in. Instead of regular panties, Lauren chose a silk thong that she had bought from Victoria's Secret awhile back. She then applied peach-scented body spray to her neck and wrists and put on a tight jean catsuit.

Lauren stared at herself in the mirror for another five minutes until she was satisfied. She then went to the kitchen to check on the food in the oven. She felt like a teenager waiting on her date. Giving it some thought, she felt silly.

When the doorbell rang, the butterflies in her stomach were at their worst. She ran back to the mirror to make sure everything was perfect.

Walking to the front door, she took a deep breath before speaking. "Who is it?" Lauren asked.

"It's Bobby."

Lauren opened the door and Bobby stood there with a dish in his hand. "Come on in."

Once Bobby was inside he said, "Since you're health conscious, I brought you a fruit salad. I make a mean banana pudding, but it's about a thousand calories."

"My goodness. No, thank you. The fruit salad is fine."

"It smells good in here. What are you cooking?"

"My specialty. Vegetarian lasagna."

"Sounds interesting."

"You'll like it. Come on, let's go in the kitchen."

Bobby followed her to the kitchen and sat down at the table.

"You have a beautiful home."

"Thank you."

Then she said, "So tell me something about yourself."

"There's really nothing much to tell. I have a small business, selling communication devices. Divorced, one child."

"How old is your child?"

"She's nineteen. She's in school at Central."

"What is she majoring in?"

"Pre-law."

"I know you're proud of her."

"Yeah, that's my heart."

As Lauren was fixing their plates, Bobby said, "Did you ever tell Brian that you got pregnant during the first time?"

"No, I never told him. We never really communicated much, especially after we married."

"Oh."

"It's funny how I fell in love with a sharing and wonderful man, but I married someone else. I never understood what went wrong, but now I know."

Bobby cast his eyes to the ceiling.

Lauren said, "Why didn't you just tell me?"

"'Cause of Brad. I was under the impression that Brian was his father, so I didn't want to complicate things."

"I feel so used. It's like I got the raw end of the deal."

"I feel the same way. You can't begin to imagine what I went through. It made me sick to my stomach to even be around you, not being able to get over you."

Lauren handed him a plate. "And now?"

"Now what?"

"Are you sick on the stomach?"

"I mean, I'm here. But still."

"Still what?"

"Our status remains the same."

"Before or after Brian?"

"After Brian."

"Is that the way you want it?"

"I just want to be happy."

"Me too."

"It's been a long time."

Lauren smiled. "Since what?"

"Since a lot of things. Where do I start?"

Lauren got up and walked over to him. She sat in his lap and said, "I say start somewhere that'll make both of us happy at the same time."

*　　　*　　　*

L tossed and turned until he finally gave up on getting some sleep. Rome's funeral was in eight hours and he still didn't know if he was going. He eased out of the bed and put on his clothes. The clock read 3:12 a.m.

He drove to one of the few places where he could buy liquor at this time of morning. Goldey's liquor house was one of the most popular places for the civilized urban crowd to hang out. It was a place where you could gamble, drink, and get a great chicken sandwich at any hour.

Goldey was an ex big-time drug dealer/gangster who had once terrorized Durham for thirty years. When Goldey decided that he was getting too old for that, he believed that opening a liquor house would be the perfect retirement plan. He had acquired his name because no matter what his mood was he always smiled, revealing a gold tooth.

As soon as L came within three blocks of the liquor house, he knew that it was packed because the streets came to life. He even had to drive a block away just to find a parking spot. After walking to the liquor house, he paid Jimmy the doorman a five-dollar admission fee and went in. He went straight to the bar.

"What can I get for you?" asked the bartender.

"Let me get a fifth of Seagrams."

"We don't sell it like that. We sell it by the glass."

"Well, add up how many glasses will go in a fifth and charge me for the shit." The bartender hesitated.

L went into a rage. "What the fuck! You stupid or something? You can't add?"

Just then, an older but physically fit man walked up. "What's going on, Mookie?"

L looked back to see who had the nerve to play hero. A brown-skinned man was smiling at him. He wore a black T-shirt with *RIP Santonio Parker* printed in white letters.

"Goldey, this guy wants to buy a whole fifth of Seagrams, and I told him that we don't sell it like that."

Goldey studied L for a moment before saying, "Give it to him for a buck."

"Okay," Mookie said as he went to get the bottle.

Goldey looked back to L. "You okay now?"

"Yeah, I'm good."

"Okay now." Goldey walked off.

L saw *RUN Jason Parker* printed on the back of the shirt. After L paid for the gin, he spun around on the stool and observed the activities. There were some familiar faces there, but he knew no one personally. So when a familiar man walked up, L didn't mind.

"L? Is that you, my nigga?"

"Come on, Peter Rabbit. You know this me." The men shook hands.

Peter Rabbit sat down beside him and in a slow drawl said, "I don't mind if I do have a seat."

L smiled. Peter Rabbit was known to clown.

He said, "Yeah, man. I heard about what happened to your boy Rome. That's fucked up, too, 'cause he was a good nigga."

L just nodded.

Peter Rabbit saw the bottle in L's hand and flagged down the bartender.

"What's up, P.R.?"

"Man, I told you to stop calling me that bullshit. That shit sounds gay as fuck."

Mookie laughed. "My fault. I forgot. What's up, Peter Rabbit?"

"Let me get a cup."

Mookie gave him a paper cup.

Peter Rabbit held it out to L. "Pour me a taste of that, baby boy."

L poured him some and said, "I see that nigga Goldey got them cousins on his shirt. He used to fuck with them niggas or something?"

"Yeah. Them niggas used to be here all the time until they got fucked up."

"I just read a book about them."

"Their whole story revolves around me. How the fuck that

ignorant-ass author gonna give me just one scene? I'm the one that first put them niggas on with the dope."

L started laughing. "You stunting like a muthafucka."

Peter Rabbit paused for a second. "Yeah, I'm stunting. But, still, I did use to roll with them niggas. 'Da Kiss' bag's shitted on all the competition for a minute. Them other niggas couldn't sell shit around here. I'm telling you, man, them niggas were like gods around here."

The men talked and drank until the bottle was gone. L flagged down the bartender again.

"What's up, killer?"

"Let me get another bottle."

Mookie wanted to say that Goldey had to approve it, but the look in L's face made him think twice.

L pulled out a wad of money and paid Mookie.

An older lady walked up and said, "Peter Rabbit, let me speak to you for a moment. Please."

Peter Rabbit tore his eyes off the money that was hanging out of L's pocket and looked at the lady. "L, I'll be right back. Don't go nowhere. got to tell you something." L nodded.

Mookie brought L the second bottle, and L began to drink again.

Three minutes later, Peter Rabbit returned and sat beside L. "Them hoes can't get enough of this dick. I believe it has a distinctive taste that seasons their food when they eat."

L laughed. "You stupid." He refilled Peter Rabbit's cup and slurred, "You're a'ight with me."

Peter Rabbit glanced at the money again. "Sheeit. Then you don't mind throwing a nigga a couple of dollars so I can cop me a bag. I'm trying to slide off with this broad."

"You still fuck with that heroin? That shit gonna kill you, man."

"Man, I ain't trying to hear that shit. I'm dope-sick, so just look out."

"Nah, dick. I don't support nobody's habit."

"You serious?" Peter Rabbit asked, frowning. "All that money you got on you and you can't break a nigga off?"

"Don't worry about how much money I got. You better be happy with that liquor."

Feeling drunk and violent, Peter Rabbit slammed the cup of liquor on the floor. Then he stood and and towered over L, who was still sitting. "You ain't gonna handle me like that. You need to let me get something," he said, cutting his eye at the money hanging out of L's pocket.

L laughed again. "Man, you better sit your dope-fiending ass down. That liq's got you talking out of your head."

"Fiending? Why I got to fiend when I got your money?" In a quick motion, he snatched at the money. To Peter Rabbit's surprise, L caught his wrist and held it with a vise-like grip. Peter Rabbit threw a short right hook that caught L on the chin.

Still holding on to Peter Rabbit's wrist, L fell to the floor. As Peter Rabbit began to stomp him, L reached under his shirt and pulled out a semi-automatic handgun.

Peter Rabbit saw the gun and screamed, "Lord Jesus Christ! I'm sorry!"

L squeezed off two shots that struck Peter Rabbit in the stomach and side. Peter Rabbit collapsed and L jumped to his feet. People were screaming and running for the exit. Out of the corner of L's eye, he saw Mookie reaching for something, so he spun toward him and fired three times.

With his adrenaline pumping and his blood boiling, he turned back to finish Peter Rabbit off and heard the report of an assault rifle. L took off running and dove out the nearest window. When he hit the ground and looked up, he saw Goldey sticking an AK-47 out the window. Before the AK spat the remainder of its twenty-seven shots, L was up and running in the opposite direction of his car.

*   *   *

"What! You giving up on Grip?" Erica asked Shawnda.

"Yeah, bitch. I'm tired of chasing his ass. I'm just tired of Durham period. Everybody's dying and shit. All these niggas want to do is get high … and beef. Look at how pitiful that funeral was — wasn't even no ballers there. I wasted my time and money on a dress." She walked over to Erica's living room window.

"You kept the receipt, right?"

"Yeah, I got it."

"Take it back then."

"You already know that, but still. This place is depressing.

That's why I'm leaving in two weeks."

"Where you going?"

"To New Orleans. I got an aunt that lives down there in a big-ass house."

"Yeah?"

"Yeah. She's sick and needs somebody to take care of her."

"Girl, I know that's your aunt and all, but you going all the way down there just to be a nurse?"

"Hell nah. I'm going down there 'cause she's about to die. And being that she ain't got no kids, and I'm her favorite niece, I know she gonna leave me everything. Bitch, I'm about to go down there and set up. I ain't got no kids, either, sheeit. I'm about to get my swerve on."

Damn she's lucky, Erica thought. She thought about her own situation. Two kids, unemployed, and an abusive boyfriend that was broke. She wished that she were in Shawnda's shoes. New Orleans wasn't exactly the fantasy place she had dreamed about, but anywhere out of the state was better than Durham.

"Erica!" Shawnda said for the third time.

"Huh?"

"Didn't you hear me? Your baby's daddy just pulled up."

Erica looked and saw Manus. "He sho' took his time getting here."

"Go get your money, bitch. Juice that nigga. That's my get-back for Grip bullshitting."

Erica got up and walked out to the Camry. "Where's Lil' Charles, with Grip?" Erica asked Manus.

"Nah, he with my girl shopping."

Jealously manifested. "Don't be leaving my son with them bitches. Ain't no telling what she might do to him if she got mad at you."

"Chill out. He's in good hands. Now what's up? You said you had something important to talk to me about."

"Let me get in." Before she got in, she looked back at Shawnda and stuck out her tongue. Once she was in the car she said, "Listen, Manus. I appreciate how you stepped up and took care of your re-sponsibilities like a man. Lil' Charles's whole attitude has changed since you came into his life. You're a blessing."

"'Preciate it."

"When I called you this morning and told you to come over, my intentions were to tell you that I was taking out child support on you."

"Child support! For what? Ever since I found out Lil' Charles was mine, I bought him everything he needed."

"That's just the thing. You bought Lil' Charles everything he needed. What about me and Kandis? We don't got shit."

Manus dropped his head and laughed. He wanted to choke her.

Erica said, "Believe it or not, I'm a good person. And that's why I'm not going to put that kind of pressure on you. Matter of fact, I'm willing to let him move in with you and give you full custody of him since y'all get along so well."

Manus knew that there had to be a catch. "I'm listening."

"I'm trying to accomplish something in life. I can't depend on Charles for shit. So I'll let you get Lil' Charles for ten thousand dollars."

"Ten thousand dollars! Are you crazy?"

"Nah, I'm far from that."

"You *something*."

"Look, Manus. I hate to be like this, but I got to look out for myself. So if you don't do that for me, I'll take out child support and keep Lil' Charles away from you by telling the judge that you are a violent felon."

Manus stared at her with a murderous look.

She continued. "I know you think I'm trying to sell you Lil' Charles and that I'm blackmailing you, but it ain't like that. I feel like I'm blessing you with the flesh and blood that you never knew about, and now I'm asking you to bless me."

Manus knew that his son was worth every penny that she was asking for, but the issue was the money. He didn't know where he was going to get the money from. He hadn't seen ten thousand dollars since before prison. Manus also knew that trying to fight Erica for custody would be useless because he was an ex-felon, and Erica hadn't done anything in the eyes of a court that suggested neglect. And in the end, his attorney's fees would add up to as much as she was now asking him for. "What happened to you while I was locked?"

"I grew up," she said as she opened the car door. "I'll give you a week to get that money up."

*   *   *

After leaving Rome's funeral, Gloria called and asked Tasha to meet her. By the time Gloria made it home, Tasha was pulling up also.

"What's up, girl? Tasha asked.

"Nothing. Need a blunt."

"It wasn't that bad, was it?"

"More pitiful than anything. Wasn't hardly nobody there."

"Uhn uhn."

"Yeah, girl. But you should've seen Rome's babies' mommas."

"What they were doing, fighting?"

"No. They were having a contest over who could cry the loudest. That shit was a trip."

Gloria unlocked the house door and went in. "Maybe they were really hurting."

"If they were, it wasn't 'cause they missed him. They're hurting 'cause that easy money is gone."

"All women aren't like that."

Gloria looked at her friend with a frown. "You a'ight? You been acting real sentimental lately."

"Have I?"

"Yeah."

"Oh. So how did L take it?"

"He wasn't even there. When I woke up this morning he was gone."

"Oh."

"Yeah, girl. He took it real bad, though. Him and Rome been friends forever."

All of a sudden Tasha burst out crying.

Gloria said, "I don't know what you're crying for. You didn't even like Rome like that."

"I ain't crying over Rome. I'm crying over the whole situation. I just wish that Meat and L would just squash all that bullshit. I'm sick of it."

"Me, too, girl. But you know how niggas are with that pride shit. They would rather die than call a truce."

Tasha rubbed her stomach. "I'm just scared that Meat won't be around to see the baby born."

"What? You pregnant?"

"Five months."

"Five months! Why you ain't been told me?"

"'Cause Meat wanted to keep it on the low. He ain't want L to try to capitalize on it."

"But I'm your —" Gloria got quiet when she saw L watching them from the hallway.

*   *   *

Manus walked in the house and slammed the door behind him. He was furious. "Stinking-ass bitch!" he yelled. "I should murk her ass." He went to Grip's liquor cabinet and grabbed a bottle of E&J. After he poured himself a drink, he put the bottle back and just stared in the glass.

At that very moment, he hated Erica more than anything he had ever hated in his life. He couldn't believe she was blackmailing him. Ten thousand dollars! He didn't know how he was going to get that kind of money in a week.

He loved his son more than anything, and he knew that Lil' Charles would rather live with him than Erica. That is what hurt Manus the most.

Manus knew that if he didn't provide for and love his son as Big Leet had for him, he would never measure up to his father. Manus abandoned his drink and went to the house phone. He located Mark's number in his cell phone and dialed it on the house phone.

Mark answered on the first ring. "Hello?"

"That's fucked up, nigga."

"Who this?"

"This Manus; don't hang up."

"I ain't going to hang up. What's good with you?"

"My muthafucking money."

"You shouldn't even be mad at me; you slipped. Charge it to the game."

"Nigga, I was trying to look out for you, and this is how you going to handle me?"

"How was you looking out for me? You don't know me from Adam. Just look at this as a lesson; it could have been for more. Holla back."

The line went dead.

Manus dialed the number again, but decided to terminate on the first ring. Even though he was mad, he received the lesson from Mark. He just had to forget about the obstacles and focus on opportunities. And in one way or another, Manus knew that he would come up with the ten thousand dollars.

CHAPTER 22

Grip helped Six pull the enormous fish onto the boat. It was obvious that it was larger than the one Grip had caught, so he handed Six a roll of money. "Lucky catch."

"Call it what you want," Six boasted. "This is what I do. Matter of fact, I don't even think I had any bait on my hook."

Grip laughed. "You're full of it."

"Maybe we should bet on who'll catch the smallest fish?" The men laughed.

Grip cut his laughter short when he noticed two white men, whom he'd seen at the hotel, looking at him. The men had on dark shades and Bermuda shorts that had been purchased at the hotel's souvenir store. But what made Grip the most suspicious were their dark dress socks and shoes. Every time he looked at them, they were watching him.

Out of the blue Six said, "Do you miss the game?"

Grip frowned and looked back at the white men. They turned their heads. Fed up, Grip turned to Six. "Six, what's going on?"

"What do you mean?"

"Come on, Six. I know you. Something is going on."

Six glanced back and sighed. "It's that obvious, huh?"

Grip nodded.

"L got me fucked up, and now I'm running."

*   *   *

"Hey, baby. I ain't know you were back there."

L ignored Gloria and looked at Tasha. "Five months, huh?"

Tasha didn't respond.

Gloria said, "Baby, where's your car?"

"Shut the fuck up!" Then he said to Tasha, "You been fucking with that nigga the whole time, haven't you?"

"L, I been messing with that man way before any of that bullshit started. So I don't know what you're talking about."

"You know what the fuck I'm talking about. You playing both sides!"

"I don't got shit to do with what y'all are going through."

"You got everything to do with it." L walked over to her and grabbed her by the hair.

"No, L!" Gloria screamed. "She's pregnant."

"Even better."

Tasha struggled with him, but L easily overpowered her and threw her to the floor. She broke her fall with her arm and screamed, "Gloria, help me!"

Gloria ran behind L and grabbed him. She smelled the liquor seeping through his pores. "Please stop, L. You're drunk!"

L pulled out his gun and smacked Gloria in the face with it. She fell and hit her head on the side of the coffee table. He then pointed the gun at Tasha. "Now where that nigga stay at?"

*   *   *

"What do you mean you're *running*?" Grip asked. "The Feds are looking for you?"

Six held up his hand. "Nah, it ain't nothing like that."

"What is it then?"

"A while back, I sent L to serve a customer of mine. He came back about an hour and a half later talking about the police had the meeting spot flooded when he got there. I got a call later on from this guy that calls himself Amado. This guy, Amado, accused me of setting his peoples up."

"With the police?"

"Nah, they were robbed and murdered."

"Goddamn!"

"I know."

"So he believes you had something to do with it?"

Six nodded.

Grip said, "So you asked L about it again, right?"

"Yeah."

"And what he say?"

"He basically stuck to his story. But he mentioned that his boys rode with him for protection."

"You believe he done it?"

"Hell yeah. I know he did it 'cause he says he got there on time, which was at six. But he didn't get back to my house until like seven-twenty. Now you tell me what the hell he was doing for an hour and a half."

"Why didn't you just give them up to the dude and be done with it?"

"I tried, but he wasn't trying to hear nothing. He told me that it was still my fault 'cause I sent L."

"Damn, Six."

"I don't know what to do. This muthafucka keep threatening my life and shit."

"It's been a minute now and he ain't done nothing. Maybe he was just talking?"

"I wish. He's the one that killed L's boy, Tee."

"Nah. Manus was there that night. He said that the guy that L and them was fighting did it."

The whole time Grip was disagreeing, Six was shaking his head no. "The same night that Tee got killed, Amado called my house and said something that let me know he done it. That's when I really cut L off. I haven't made any moves since then." Six paused to wipe his brow with a handkerchief. "That muthafucka called my house again the day before you called me about this trip. That nigga is driving me crazy."

"Why don't you just get the guy dealt with?"

"I've tried that, but my guy can't find him. Dude's like a ghost. All of my amigo friends have heard of him but couldn't tell me nothing about him … other than he's José's enforcer."

"Who's José?"

"One of the dudes that got killed."

Grip dropped his fishing rod and reached into his pocket. "Oh shit! I've got to warn Manus."

*   *   *

Meat sat in his apartment and watched the twelve o'clock news. At any time, he was expecting to see his face on TV. When the local news came on he turned the volume up.

"Durham police are investigating a shooting that left one man dead and another in critical condition. Marion Thompson is standing by with a report. Marion?"

The studio cut to a woman standing in front of Goldey's liquor house with an officer. "This is Marion Thompson reporting live from the eleven hundred block of Coleman Street, where Samual "Mookie" Perry was shot to death, and another man seriously injured. I'm standing here with Officer Mickely." She turned to him, "Can you tell us what happened?"

"Marion, this is an illegal gambling house. From what we have gathered, a male in the house was gambling and lost his money. He apparently demanded it back because he felt cheated. When that didn't happen, it resulted in two men being shot."

"This makes the forty-third murder this year, and we're only in the ninth month. What can be done to prevent these murders?"

"The community can get more involved in their neighborhoods. The power of neighborhood watch will make criminals think twice before pulling the trigger."

"Well, good luck on solving the case, Officer Mickely."

"Thank you."

"This is Marion Thompson reporting live from Coleman Street. Back to you, Dan."

The scene cut to the news studio. "Thank you, Marion. As you can see," he said to the viewers, "Durham police have their hands full. The suspect is described as a six-foot black man with reddish hair." He looked down at the papers in front of him. "Durham police still do not have any suspects in the shooting death of a man at the Red Roof Inn three days ago. Police found thirty-year-old Romel Bass shot to death in the elevator of the hotel. Anybody with any information about this murder, or the one on Coleman Street, please call 1-800-Crime Stoppers. There's a twelve-hundred-dollar reward for anybody with information leading to the arrest and conviction of the suspect."

Meat turned off the TV, relieved that he was still in the clear. He thought about the rough description of the man that was suspected in the shootings at Goldey's. Meat knew that there weren't a lot of black men around there with red hair. He sat back and smiled.

*   *   *

Manus muted the TV and dialed L's cell phone number.

L answered, breathing hard. "Yo?"

"What's the deal, man? You good?"

"Yeah. What's good?"

"Not shit. Just seen some crazy shit on the news that happened at —" Screaming could be heard in the background. "The fuck you doing?" Manus asked.

"I'mma hit you back."

The line went dead.

Manus set the phone down and it instantly began to ring. "Yeah?"

"Where are you?" Grip asked.

"At home. What's up?"

"Remember what you asked me about Six?"

"Yeah."

"Well, he just told me what's up, and your boy ain't right."

"Who, L?"

"Yeah."

"What's up with him?"

"He jerked some of Six's Mexican peoples and now it's something like a hit on him. I want you to stay away from that guy. The Mexican guy ain't playing. You know what happened to Tee, right?"

"Yeah."

"Well, that's his work."

"Nah, Unc. The dude that they —"

"I know that's what you thought, but he didn't do it. Trust me. Stay away from L. I don't want you to get caught up in that shit. You hear me?"

"Yeah, I hear you."

"Matter of fact, just lay low for a few days. I heard that something else might be about to go down."

"I will."

"You sound funny; is everything okay back there?"

"Just some crazy stuff that Erica is trying to pull."

"What is she trying to do?"

"It ain't nothing that I can't handle. Gone and enjoy yourself; I'm straight."

"You sure?"

"Yeah, I'm sure."

"See you in a couple of days."

"A'ight, Unc."

*   *   *

Grip pressed *END* on his cell phone and looked at Six. "It's a done deal."

"What did he say?"

"He thought that it was the other guy that killed him. But he gonna stay away from L."

"That's a good thing."

"Yeah. Manus ... Oh shit!" Grip's whole body tensed up when he saw one of the two white men pull out a pair of handcuffs.

"What?" Six asked.

"Don't look, but something is up with them two white guys. First I seen them at the hotel, and now here. It's like they're following us or something."

"I already know who you're talking about. Every time I look they're staring at us."

"Do you think it's the peoples? I just seen one of them pull out a pair of cuffs."

"Man, I don't know. I hope not."

"Oh shit!"

"What?"

"They're coming over here."

"I can't go to prison, Grip."

Grip turned to Six sharply.

The white men walked up to them, and the tall one said, "Excuse me."

Grip said, "What's up?"

"I'm Jack, and this is my partner Fred. We've been watching you gentlemen all day."

Grip looked around for an escape route, but they were in the middle of the ocean. Jack continued, "We were wondering if you and your man friend would like to join us tonight for a little fun and games?"

*   *   *

"I don't know where he stay at," Tasha said.

L cocked the hammer back on his gun. "You think I'm playing, bitch? I'mma ask you one more time."

"I ain't never been to his house!" Tasha silently prayed that she would survive this. She needed Meat. But she couldn't live with herself if she was the cause of him being killed.

L glared at her for a long period. Not being able to tell whether she was lying, he stomped her in the stomach out of frustration.

Tasha balled up and clutched her stomach. "Oww! My baby, L!"

"You think I give a fuck about that muthafuckin bastard?" He kicked Tasha viciously in the back.

Tasha screamed, "Help me, Gloria!"

L took his attention off Tasha and looked back at Gloria. She lay motionless on the floor where she had fallen. "Gloria, get your ass up. Ain't shit wrong with you." When she didn't respond, L walked over and rolled her over. He noticed that her neck looked awkward. "Baby, wake up. Baby!"

When Tasha saw that her friend was unresponsive, she screamed, "Oh my God! You killed her!"

"No, Gloria, please!" L buried his face between Gloria's breasts and sobbed. "I swear I ain't mean to. I swear."

Tasha saw the opportunity and got to her feet. She knew that if she stayed she would never see Meat again. This thought alone motivated her. As soon as she got to the door and opened it, L turned and fired two shots. He got up, scurrying, and stepped over Tasha's body to close the door again. Then he went back to Gloria and felt her neck for a pulse, just in case. When he didn't find one, he collapsed beside her and wept.

CHAPTER 23

Manus ended his call with Grip and was disappointed with L. He now knew what L and Rome's second hustle was. Although he had nothing against people who got their money through robbing, he certainly had a problem with people that robbed the hand that fed them.

Manus knew that their robbing Six suggested that everyone was fair game, himself included. But through all of this, he didn't see L as the enemy. He felt obligated to at least tell L about the killer that was after him. He dialed L's number, but the phone just rang. Deciding to call him back later, he got in the shower. As soon as he did, he heard his cell phone ringing. Soaking wet, Manus answered the phone. "Hello?"

"Hey, Manus. This is Lauren."

"Hey, Ms. Lauren. How you doing?"

"I'm doing much better now. How about yourself?"

"I'm okay."

"What are you doing today?"

"I don't have anything planned. My girlfriend took my son shopping. Why, what's up?"

"Do you want to come over here for dinner?"

"I sure would."

Lauren laughed. "Good, because I want you to meet somebody. Actually, two people."

"Okay, what time?"

"In an hour."

"I'll be there."

"See you then."

Manus ended the call wishing Lil' Charles was there so that he could take him to meet Lauren. Lil' Charles and Gee had become close lately. Gee had told Manus that Lil' Charles was her preparation for motherhood. Manus thought it was a bold statement. He didn't know if he was ready for another kid.

*   *   *

Six and Grip looked at one another and started laughing. They laughed so hard that the white men began to laugh also.

After the laughter subsided Grip said, "Sorry, doc, but we're both straight as can be."

Jack observed how soft spoken and polite Grip was and decided to try his hand. "You only live once, so don't limit your experiences."

Grip quickly stood. "You better get your muthafuckin ass away from here before I throw both of your feminine asses off this boat!"

Jack and Fred quickly retreated to their seats.

Six and Grip looked at one another and began to laugh again.

*   *   *

When Manus pulled up at Lauren's house, he saw a Volvo parked behind Lauren's car.

Lauren answered the door and gave him a hug. "Hey, Manus."

"Hey, Ms. Lauren. *Uhmm*, I smell it from here."

"It's ready. Come on in. I want you to meet somebody," Lauren said as she took his hand. When they reached the den, Manus saw a man sitting on the couch.

The man stood, and Lauren said, "Manus, this is Bobby Anderson. Bobby, this is Manus."

The men shook hands. Manus stared at the man and tried to figure out where he knew him from. Then it came to him. "You're Brad's uncle, right? I seen some pictures of you and Brad's dad."

Lauren said, "Sit down, Manus. This is one of the persons who I wanted you to meet."

The men sat down. Lauren explained to Manus all about her situation with Bobby and Brian.

After she finished, Manus said, "Whoa." Then he stood and shook Bobby's hand again. "I'm honored to meet you. Brad was a good dude."

Just then, the doorbell rang. Lauren got up. "That must be Demetrius." She walked out of the room and returned a minute later with a new guest. Lauren said, "I want y'all to meet Demetrius. Demetrius, meet Bobby and Manus."

Manus' heart dropped when he was introduced to Meat.

*   *   *

Not being able to find L had clearly frustrated Amado. Since Tee's death, L had been underground. But not much time had passed before Amado finally got his break. While watching the news, he had seen Rome's face. After learning that Rome had been murdered, Amado knew that that was his chance to settle things once and for all. For the next few days, Amado had bought newspapers to find out where the funeral services would be held. On the second day, Rome's picture turned up in the obituaries. On the day of the wake, Amado sat in the funeral home and waited for L. When he failed to show up, Amado figured that he would show up at the funeral. As he sat in the parking lot on the day of the funeral, two women in a car next to him seemed to be waiting for someone also. Their conversation could be heard over the sweet sounds of Selena.

"Oh no, she don't got on the same skirt she had on at the club Friday," the woman said, referring to another woman that was going into the funeral home. "All the pussy she be slinging, she suppose to be in something exclusive."

"And her own limo," the other woman had added.

"Hell yeah."

Then a green Malibu pulled into the parking lot. One woman said, "Oww, look, bitch!"

"What?"

"See that bitch driving the green car?"

"Yeah."

"She's the one that fucks with L."

Erica observed the woman getting out of her car. "I ain't never seen her before. What's her name?"

"Gloria. I can't stand her ass, either."

"I like her man, though, bitch."

"I wonder why he ain't with her."

Amado had turned the sounds of Selena all the way down and observed the woman in the Malibu. He'd also leaned back on the car seat and formed a plan B.

*   *   *

L opened his eyes and wondered how long he had been asleep. He looked at Gloria's corpse and started crying again. "I'm so sorry, baby," he said, stroking her cheek.

Knowing he had to get things together, he got up to retrieve the heavy-duty trash bags from the kitchen. L stopped at the kitchen's doorway and looked back. To his surprise and horror, the front door was ajar and Tasha was gone. L ran to the door and looked out. He saw an ambulance and three police cars four houses down. He quickly walked out of the house and went to Gloria's car.

*   *   *

Tasha opened her eyes and felt an excruciating pain in her back. She looked back and saw L lying motionless beside Gloria. She thought he was dead until he stirred. Tasha struggled to her feet and slowly turned the doorknob.

Once she was outside, Tasha struggled to reach next door as fast as her weak and wobbly legs would carry her. When no one answered the neighbor's door, she tried the next one and so on until she got an answer.

A small white lady answered the fourth door.

Tasha could barely say, "Please help me. I've been shot."

"Oh my God!" The white lady said as she helped her inside. She sat Tasha on the couch and picked up the cordless phone. After she hung up with the dispatcher, Tasha grabbed the phone and began dialing.

*   *   *

When Manus saw Meat, he jumped to his feet.

Meat took a couple of steps backward and reached under his

shirt.

Startled and confused, Lauren said, "What's wrong?"

Manus looked at Meat and then at the window.

Meat recollected himself. "What is he doing here?"

Lauren said, "This is Brad's —"

"I know who he is, but I don't think you do."

Remembering what Meat had done to Rome, Manus watched the hand under the shirt.

"What's going on with you two? Do you know each other?"

"Yeah, I know him," Meat said, glaring at Manus. "But I'll let him tell you how."

Lauren looked at Manus. "What's going on, Manus?"

Manus held his hands at shoulder length. "I know what you're thinking, but it ain't even like that."

Lauren looked from man to man. "Somebody better tell me something."

Manus said, "Some guy that I used to deal with —"

"Oh, now you *used to* deal with him?" Meat asked, cutting him off.

"Listen, rap, let me explain."

"Really, it ain't nothing you can say."

Getting frustrated, Manus said, "Rap, whatever you're thinking, I still don't got nothing to do with none of that stuff."

"You got everything to do with everything, especially when you're up in Ms. Lauren's face like everything's kosher!"

Tired of the bickering, Lauren said, "Demetrius, just forget about Manus for a moment. I want you to tell me what the problem is."

Meat took a deep breath. "That nigga be around the nigga that ki —" Meat's phone started ringing. "Hello?"

"Baby," Tasha said weakly. "I got shot."

"What!"

"L shot me."

"Where are you at?"

Tasha began to sob hard. "I haven't felt the baby move. I think something is wrong with him."

"Where are you at?"

"I can't breathe. I ..."

Meat heard the phone drop to the floor. "Hello? Hello?"

Moments later, a woman came on the line. "Hello?"

"Where's Tasha?"

"She passed out, but the ambulance is here."

"What hospital are y'all near?"

"Durham Regional."

Meat ended the call and ran out of the house.

* * *

Amado sat in the car and watched the house from forty yards away. He was beginning to feel restless until he saw an apparently crippled woman come out of the house and begin to struggle toward the next house. Wondering what was going on, he kept looking back at the house but saw nothing.

When the crippled woman was at the fourth house, he saw a white lady assisting her. Amado knew that within minutes the whole street would be swarming with police, but he forced himself to stay awhile longer. He wasn't about to let the woman, who had arrived earlier in the Malibu, get out of his sight.

Two minutes after police and an ambulance arrived, to Amado's surprise, he saw L walk out of the house and get in the Malibu. He allowed a casual head start before he trailed him.

* * *

"Put it in my ass," Shawnda said to Dread.

Dread withdrew from her vagina and entered her rectum. It seemed to suck him in. "Ohh."

"Do it hard," she demanded.

Dread pushed her legs behind her head and began to stroke violently. Shawnda reached back and grabbed the headboard to prevent it from knocking against the wall. She let out an occasional moan, but overall she was silent.

After Dread climaxed, he rolled off of her and began to rub her stomach. "You got to start eating more. That baby is smaller than a muthafucka."

She grabbed his hand. "Dread, we got to talk."

"About what?"

"About the baby."

"What about him? Is he okay?"

"Nah, I lost him the day before yesterday."

Dread sat up abruptly. "How?"

"I don't know how. The doctor don't, either."

"But how you have a miscarriage and you ain't bleeding now?"

"Because all women don't bleed when they miscarry, crazy."

"Oh, I ain't know." Dread flopped back onto the bed in frustration. "I must have bad luck or something, 'cause that's the third baby that we've lost."

"It ain't that. Maybe our genes or something ain't right together. I bet you can get another bitch pregnant quick."

"I don't want no babies by nobody else. I want them by you. And I ain't gonna give up 'til I do."

"Dread. I got to tell you something else, too."

"What, baby?"

"I'm moving to New Orleans in a couple of weeks."

Dread sat back up. "What!"

"My aunt is real sick and don't got nobody —"

In a swift motion, Dread grabbed her by the neck and slammed her head into the headboard. "You trying to fucking play me?"

"Nigga, you better take your muthafuckin hands off me!"

They locked eyes for a moment before Dread released her. "I wasn't gonna say nothing," he said, breathing hard, "but I know about that nigga at Erica's house today."

"What nigga?"

"That nigga pushing that old-ass Camry. My peoples told me. Let me find out that's who you're leaving me for. I'll tint his windows with his brains."

"Crazy, that's Erica's baby's daddy!"

"I know Charles! That powder-snorting-ass nigga ain't got no goddamn car. Who the fuck you think you're talking to?"

"Bitch, Erica got two baby daddies. Charles and Manus."

"Manus? Manus who?"

"I can't remember his real name, but he got a uncle named Grip."

"You talking about Grip with the detail shop?"

"Yeah, crazy."

"I ain't know Erica had a baby by Manus."

"Yeah, her oldest child is his."

"*Yesss,* sir," Dread said softly.

* * *

When L pulled up to a gated community called the Atrium, he stopped at a box and punched in a code. The gate opened and he drove through. The gate closed again.

Amado pulled up five seconds later and swore aloud when he saw the code box and the gate. It crossed his mind to jump the gate, but he decided against it when he saw cameras at various angles. Amado knew that if he jumped the gate the police would be there within minutes looking for him. He didn't need the heat. He drove across the street to Carver Ponds apartments and waited. He was focused.

* * *

Meat ran inside the emergency room and went straight to the desk that had a blonde working a computer. "I need to find out where Latasha Umstead is at!"

"Latasha who?"

"Umstead. Latasha Umstead."

"Okay." She typed the name into the computer. "I'm sorry, sir, but the computer is not showing anybody by that name here."

"Check again, ma'am. I know they brought her here."

"Who are 'they'?"

"The goddamn ambulance!"

The blonde began to type again, and moments later she shook her head. "I'm sorry, sir. But the computer just isn't showing anything on that name. Are you sure that's her name?"

Meat bit his bottom lip and balled up his fists. Then he heard a commotion to his right and saw two paramedics pushing a gurney through the sliding double doors. Meat rushed toward them and saw Tasha, who was unconscious. She lay on her side with nothing on but her bra and pants.

"Baby! Baby!"

One of the paramedics tried to prevent Meat from touching

Tasha, but Meat snatched away from him.

"You better get your muthafucking hands off me; that's my girl!"

"Sir, you're in the way. We're trying to save her life."

A doctor ran up, took one look at Tasha, and started screaming orders.

They began to push the gurney through another set of doors.

Meat tried to follow them, but a nurse stopped him. "I'm sorry, sir. But you are going to have to wait here."

"But I'm her fiancé."

"I understand that, but there's nothing that you can do in there but get in the way."

"I'll stay out of the way," he said as he attempted to go around the nurse.

The nurse blocked his path. "Sir, you're not allowed in the operating room. Please don't make me call security. Please. I'll make sure the doctor comes and talks to you as soon as possible."

"A'ight," Meat said reluctantly. "But please save them."

"We're going to do all we can."

Meat turned around and walked out of the hospital with one thing on his agenda.

CHAPTER 24

Over dinner, Manus had just told Lauren and Bobby about the whole situation with him, L, and Meat.

"So who really killed my son?"

Manus sighed. "I still don't know, Ms. Lauren. I can't just put it on L, but from the things that I've learned about him lately, I can't rule it out, either."

Bobby said, "Before that guy L knew that you were a good friend of Brad's, did he ever give any indication that he killed Brad or had something to do with it?"

"Nope. See, I only dealt with him on the business tip. We really didn't hang."

Manus saw the confused look on Lauren's face and realized his mistake.

"What kind of business?" she asked.

"Uh…"

"Your uncle's dry cleaning business?" Bobby asked.

"Yeah."

Manus glanced at Bobby and gave him a grateful look. "Yeah, my uncle's cleaners."

"Oh, I see." She put her head down and was silent.

"Don't worry, Ms. Lauren. Whoever did that to Brad ain't gonna get away with it."

"I hope not."

Bobby said, "I hope you and Demetrius can come to an understanding of some kind."

"It ain't me; it's him."

"I'll call him later and talk to him."

"Thank you," Manus said as he stood.

"You leaving so soon?"

"Yeah, I should be going."

Lauren stood and gave him a hug. "Thanks for coming to eat with us."

"Anytime."

"Now, I want you to be careful out there. Those streets are mean."

"Believe me, I will not be pulled into that nonsense."

"I'm talking about other things, too."

Catching her drift, Manus said, "I promise to be careful."

Bobby stood and shook Manus' hand. "Nice to meet you."

"You too, man."

They walked to the door and Lauren said, "Don't be a stranger."

"I won't."

As Manus walked to the car, his cell phone began to ring. "Hello?"

"Dick, what's up?"

Recognizing L's voice, Manus said, "Yo, I've been trying to hit you. Check —"

"Yo," he said, cutting him off. "I done fucked up bad. I need your help."

Manus heard the urgency in his voice. "Check. Let's just meet somewhere where we can talk, 'cause I got some serious shit to tell you that I don't want to discuss over the phone."

"It got to be now, 'cause I don't have no time to waste."

"Okay. Meet me at Ruby Tuesdays at North Gate in fifteen minutes."

"Hell nah. I can't show my face at no mall. That substation is down there. Fuck no."

"Well, meet me at Duke Park then."

"Word. That'll work. But look, though. Call your man Tree. Tell him that I know he don't fuck with me, but I need the works. S.S. and all. Tell him I'll pay him double."

"A'ight, I got you."

*   *   *

With tears in his eyes and a .40 caliber in his lap, Meat drove around the curve and saw Manus' Camry leaving Lauren's house. He grabbed the gun and accelerated. He knew that if anybody knew how to find L, Manus did.

As he tailed the car he pictured Tasha lying on the gurney, bleeding. He thought about the loss of his baby and how Manus was playing on Ms. Lauren's emotions. Meat wiped the tears from his eyes.

Manus got in the left turning lane at the red light.

Meat did not change lanes. He stopped behind two other cars. Only seven feet from Manus, Meat stared at the side of his head.

Manus was talking on the phone, oblivious to his surroundings.

Meat's plan was to find out where L was, but he found himself rolling down the window and aiming his gun. He cocked back the hammer and targeted Manus' head.

*   *   *

Dread opened his eyes and looked over at Shawnda, who was lying with her back to him. He eased out of bed and retrieved the cell phone from his pants pocket. Once he was in the bathroom, he shut the door and made a call.

"Yeah?"

"Yo, guess what?"

"What's that?"

"I just found out that ole boy got a baby by Shawnda's friend Erica."

"Who that?"

"Your boy, Manus."

"Quit bullshitting."

"Real shit. Shawnda just told me. You know how dick make them hoes spill beans."

"That makes shit so sweet."

"Who you telling. But look, though, I'll hit you back when I leave this broad's house."

"Hurry up, man, and do that."

"I am."

Dread ended the call and peeked out the door. He saw that Shawnda's back was still turned from him. He crept back to the bed and eased into it.

Shawnda closed her eyes and tried to make sense of Dread's

conversation.

*　　　*　　　*

As soon as Meat's finger curled around the trigger, quick-chirping sirens erupted behind him. Meat withdrew the gun then checked his rearview mirror. He saw a policeman rushing out of his cruiser, and positioning himself behind the door with his gun aimed.

"Driver, stick your hands out the window!"

"Goddamn," Meat mumbled. He scanned his surroundings and weighed his options. Cars in front of him made it impossible for him to run the light. To his right was the wide-open parking lot of King's grocery store. He turned the steering wheel to the right and stomped the accelerator. His fender sideswiped the car in front of him, but it didn't slow the Cherokee down as it jumped the curb. The policeman jumped back inside his cruiser to pursue the Jeep.

Meat crossed the parking lot and almost hit an old lady who was pushing a grocery cart. He jumped off the curb and zoomed into the intersection, causing an oncoming driver to slam on his brakes. Meat heard a crash, but never looked back.

As he sped up North Roxboro Road with the cruiser behind him, he knew that he had to find a place to jump out before another cruiser joined the chase. They reached speeds of up to ninety-five, and the Jeep wove in and out of traffic.

A quarter mile later, Meat slowed the Jeep and made a hard left on a narrow street. He regained control of the Jeep and looked in the rearview mirror again. Seeing that the cruiser hadn't made the turn yet, Meat took the opportunity and threw the gun out of the window. When he looked in the rearview mirror again, he saw four police cruisers, at various distances, trying to catch him.

At seventy miles per hour, the Jeep hit a small hill in the road and was off the ground. Suddenly, the street introduced a sharp curve. The Jeep's front tire landed on the curbside and exploded. Meat swerved back into the street and soon found himself flipping over with the vehicle. The Jeep veered off the street, through the fence of the Museum of Life and Science, and into a model thirty-foot brontosaurus.

When Meat regained consciousness, he was staring into the

barrels of several department-issued handguns.

*   *   *

When Manus heard the double-chirping sirens, he forgot about the caller on the phone and spun around in his seat. He saw a Cherokee jump the curb and cross the grocery store parking lot. Five seconds later, he watched a cruiser do the same thing. He shook his head. "Somebody's wilding the fuck out."

Blaring horns startled Manus, and he looked ahead to see that the light was green. Before pulling off, Manus glanced at the wreck that the chase had just caused then went on his way. Remembering that he was on the phone, he put it back to his ear. "Hello?"

"Goddamn," Tree said. "What are you doing?"

"My bad, man. I just saw a wreck. Now what was you saying?"

"I said, is it for you?"

"Nah, it's for L."

"Yo, you know I don't fuck with that nigga."

"I know, but he told me to tell you that he'll pay you double."

"I don't know. It's up to my brother. Hold on; let me ask him." He paused "Smut! Your boy L wants the ID and shit for double the price. You want to fuck with it?"

"I don't give a fuck. If he trips, I'mma..."

Tree spoke into the phone again. "Manus?"

"Yeah."

"I'll do it, but tell that nigga I ain't with no bullshit."

"Word. Good look, too."

"Matter of fact, just give that nigga my number so I can talk to him myself."

"A'ight." Manus ended the call and turned into Duke Park. The park was vacant and Manus knew he had to park and get out of the car quick. Ever since the police had found a man dead in the trunk of an abandoned car, they had been patrolling the park frequently. Manus got out and walked under the pavilion.

Five minutes later, a white Honda Accord pulled up. L got out of the car and began walking toward him.

A dark blue Taurus came around the bend, cruising slowly.

L looked back and watched the Taurus until it was out of sight.

Manus immediately noticed L's bloodshot eyes and the wild look on his face.

"What's up, dick?"

"Ain't nothing, just chilling."

"You do that for me?"

"Yeah, he told me to give you his number."

L pulled out his phone. "What is it?"

Manus gave him the number.

L stored it then pocketed the phone and sighed.

Manus knew he was distraught about something. "You a'ight?" You still fucked up about Rome?"

L dropped his head and began to tremble. "She's dead, man. I swear I didn't mean to."

"Who?"

"Gloria. Her neck, it..." He began to sob.

"Goddamn, L."

"I got to roll out. I can't stick around and let them snatch me."

"To be honest with you, leaving is the best thing you could do."

L lifted his head. "Why you say that?"

"'Cause I hollered at my uncle earlier. He told me that Six quit fucking around because you got this Mexican killer looking for y'all."

"A Mexican?"

"Yeah. He said it's the enforcer of the Mexicans you jerked."

L nodded his head solemnly as if to accept his fate. Just then, they heard the sound of someone stepping on a pine cone. Both men jerked their heads in the direction of the sound.

"Who that?" L yelled.

When there wasn't an answer, Manus continued, "All Six said was the Mexican dude was the one who killed —"

Another crackle.

L pulled out his gun and got behind a tree.

*   *   *

When the white Honda came through the gates of the Atrium Apartments, Amado immediately saw L's red hair, so he tailed him. As he did, he thought about the best way to handle the situation. Under no circumstances would he allow L to slip away this time.

It crossed his mind to pull up beside L at the light and finish him, but he decided against that. He wanted L to know why he was being murdered. It made perfect sense to kill L first because he believed L was Six's enforcer. The real threat, Six, would be easy to kill.

When L went through a yellow light at the last moment, and blended in with traffic, Amado sat at the red light in panic mode. The light finally turned green and Amado dug out. Twelve blocks later, he caught a glimpse of the Honda making a right a few streets ahead.

Amado turned onto the street and came around the bend slowly. He spotted L walking toward the pavilion. Amado casually followed the road to the other side of the park, near the playground, and parked the car. Once he was out of the car, he concealed himself behind the trees as he crept toward the men.

*   *   *

When Manus saw L pull out the gun and take cover behind a tree, Grip's warning replayed in his head. He dashed behind a tree, too, and silently prayed that it wasn't the Mexican enforcer. He knew that the guy had no intention of leaving any witnesses.

An accented voice yelled, "It's your day to die, L!"

Manus felt his knees weaken. He whispered, "You got another burner on you?"

L shook his head no and yelled, "Not today, dick. I got an appointment to make."

"Remember José, holmes? The Mexican you killed at the car wash? That was my friend, holmes."

"I ain't the one that killed José. That was my man Tee."

"And that's why I've already dealt with him."

"What! That was you that killed my mans?"

"Yeah, holmes. That running coward died a thousand deaths."

With his back to the tree, L closed his eyes and trembled. He could hear the man's laughter coming from a short distance away. In a blind fury, L came from behind the tree shooting wildly. A split second later, the report from another gun could be heard. The shooting lasted for five seconds before there was complete silence.

Manus built up the courage to look around the tree and saw L standing with his gun extended. Amado lay on the ground, motionless. Manus came from behind the tree and walked up to L. Still staring at the body, Manus said, "Goddamn, L. You a'ight?" When L didn't respond, Manus looked at him and saw that he was holding his midsection. "Oh shit! You hit!"

He helped L to the ground and pulled out his phone to call an ambulance. After he ended the call, L handed him his car keys. "Get that bag out of the trunk and give it to my momma. Tell her that I love her and to not cry for me."

"Nah, rap. Don't talk like that. You're going to make it." L closed his eyes and Manus shook him. "Stay woke, man!"

L opened his eyes. "I'm not a bad dude. The only reason I crossed Six like that is because he was ripping me off with the work. He was selling me re-rocked work."

Manus nodded and said, "Did you kill Brad?" L closed his eyes again and Manus shook him. "Stay woke, L!"

L opened his eyes. "I had every intention of killing Brad, but somebody beat me to it."

L's eyes closed again.

Manus shook him. "Stay woke, L!" When L didn't respond, Manus felt his wrist for a pulse. Manus dropped his head and remained that way for a moment. Coming to his senses, he got up and jogged to his car.

He started the car and drove off. On second thought, he stopped the car and backed up. Manus got out and went to the trunk of L's Honda. He opened it and saw a large army duffel bag. When he looked inside, he lost his breath when he saw that it was full of money.

*   *   *

Meat kicked the door of the holding cell repeatedly until a detention officer arrived.

"Sir, please stop kicking the door."

"Well let me make a goddamn phone call then!"

"Sir, you have to wait until you see the magistrate first."

"Fuck the magistrate! Y'all muthafuckas done had me in this bitch for an hour. I want my goddamn phone call!"

The detention officer saw that there was no reasoning with the inmate, so he shrugged and walked away.

Meat turned his back to the door and began kicking it again.

Sergeant Williams, who was in the back having lunch, heard the noise so she got up to see what was going on.

"Who's making all that noise?"

Three detention officers, who were working the front desk, all pointed toward the cell that held Meat.

Sergeant Williams stopped at Meat's cell door. She waited until he was in between kicks and said, "Hey!"

Meat stopped kicking the door and turned around.

When the sergeant saw him, her eyes got big. She motioned Meat to step back and he complied. She used one of her keys.

A detention officer said, "He can't make a phone call until he sees the magistrate."

The sergeant turned around. "Don't you have some paperwork that you're supposed to be doing?"

"Yes," the man said, picking up his pen.

The sergeant turned back to the holding cell and stepped in closing the door halfway behind her. "Meat, what happened to you?" she said, looking at his swollen mouth.

"Them muthafuckin police jumped on me. I need to make a phone call."

"You're not allowed to make one until after you see the magistrate. What they arrest you for?"

"Manda, fuck everything else. I'm trying to call my peoples."

"Boy, you trying to get me in trouble. You not going to take care of me if I get fired."

"I ain't trying to get you fired. I'm just trying to get in touch with my cousin, Pete."

"I understand that, but if I let you out, my job would be in jeopardy."

"Well, go in the back and call him for me."

"Okay, I can do that. What's his number?"

"555-0731. Tell him where I'm at, and tell him to come get me."

"A'ight. I'll be right back."

The sergeant left the cell and locked the door behind her.

For the first time since Meat had been in the cell, he went to the mirror and examined his face.

"Goddamn, they fucked me up."

He was now glad that he and Manda had parted on good terms. Through all the mayhem, he hadn't once thought about the fact that Manda worked at the jail.

Five minutes later, the keys turned in the lock and Manda came in with a bag of ice.

"Here, put this on your mouth."

Meat grabbed the bag of ice. "What happened?"

"I talked to him; he's on his way."

"Thanks, Manda."

"No problem, but you know you owe me, right?"

"What I owe you?"

Manda smiled, "What you're stingy with."

Meat tried to smile but his lips throbbed.

Then she said, "You're the only man that I ever met that's hard to get in bed with."

"Just call me."

"I will," she said, reaching for the door.

"Thanks again, Manda."

As Manda was leaving out the door, she yelled, "And you better not kick that door no more!"

*   *   *

Sitting in front of the magistrate's window, Meat listened as one of the arresting officers had a casual conversation with the magistrate.

"...so I told her that it must be termites."

The magistrate and officer began to laugh.

Frustrated, Meat sighed loudly. The magistrate stopped laughing and said, "Son, is there a problem?" She removed her glasses.

"Other than being beat the shit out of by four cops and being here, no."

"Officer Rankin said they had to defend themselves."

"That's some bullshit!" Meat said. "Them bastards started beating me from the jump."

The officer put his hand on Meat's shoulder.

"You better take your goddamn hands off me; you're by yourself now."

"Mr. Riley!" the magistrate said.

Meat ignored the magistrate and stood up to the officer. "What now?"

The officer looked at the magistrate. "See, I told you. This guy is out of control."

"Sit down, Mr. Riley!" the magistrate yelled.

Meat finally sat down, mumbling.

Shaking her head, the magistrate looked down at some papers and said, "You've been charged with attempted murder..."

"Bullshit."

"Felony to elude..."

"Bullshit."

"Reckless driving, hit and run, and resisting arrest. I —"

"And some more bullshit."

The magistrate looked at Meat in disgust. Then she said, "In my ten years of being a magistrate, I've never seen a character such as yourself. Officer Rankin was right; you are out of control. You haven't shown me, Officer Rankin, or yourself any respect since they brought you here. I heard you kicking the door like a madman. That doesn't make any sense. Your court date is tomorrow morning at nine o'clock on the fourth floor. I'm setting your bond at one million dollars."

CHAPTER 25

The next morning, in the courtroom, Meat sat on a bench, handcuffed to a chain and thirteen other inmates. His whole body ached from sleeping without a mattress. The detention officers had taken his after he'd cursed them out.

The guy handcuffed next to Meat whispered, "I finally figured out where I know you from. You was at the club a while back with my man Brad."

Meat simply nodded.

"God rest his soul. That was my man. We went to East End school together. Did they ever get who killed him?"

Meat shook his head.

"I'm Boo, but everybody calls me Boobie Dollars."

"Meat."

Just then, Meat's name was called. A young black man rose from the lawyers' table. "I'm Attorney Harris. I represent Mr. Riley." Then he looked at Meat and motioned for him to stand up.

The district attorney turned to the judge. "Mr. Riley has been charged with attempted murder, assault by pointing a gun, felony to elude, reckless driving, hit and run, and resisting arrest."

The judge looked over the top of his glasses. "I'm setting his next court date for November the eleventh."

Attorney Harris said, "Your Honor, I would like to request that my client's bond be lowered to a reasonable amount. It's currently at a million dollars."

The D.A. said, "Your Honor, The State asks that you deny that request. Mr. Riley is obviously a menace to society. Although a weapon wasn't recovered, the arresting officer wrote in his report that if he hadn't pulled up behind Mr. Riley, he would have committed murder."

"Your Honor, that's questionable. My client is no more a menace to society than you and I are. He has no record, and he's been to college."

The judge peered at Meat. "Are you still in school?"

"No, sir. I have plans to go back next semester, though."

"Son, I don't know where you went wrong, but I hope that you can get back focused and get a degree." He paused. "Considering that the defendant doesn't have a record, I'm going to reduce his bond to fifty thousand."

In unison, Meat and his attorney said, "Thank you, Your Honor."

Attorney Harris then looked at Meat and mouthed, "You'll be out in an hour."

*   *   *

Meat walked out of the county jail with his lawyer. "Thank you, Ryan. Take me to the house so I can get you your money."

"You don't owe me anything. Your lady friend took care of everything."

"Who?"

"Miss Grant," he said, gesturing with his head.

Meat looked and saw Tip sitting on a bench.

Ryan shook Meat's hand. "Get in touch with me so we can discuss your case."

"A'ight."

"And tell your cousin to get in touch with me also."

"A'ight. 'Preciate it."

"Anytime."

Meat walked over to Tip. "Thanks for posting my bond. How did you know?"

"It's not every day that somebody crashes into the museum's dinosaurs. It was all over the news."

"Oh. Well, take me to the crib so I can pay you back."

"Meat," she said, standing up, "I'm not concerned with the money. I'm concerned about you."

"Well, don't worry yourself too much, 'cause I'm good."

Tip lightly brushed her fingers across Meat's swollen lips. "Are you?"

Meat turned his head away.

Tip withdrew her hand. "What will it take for you to leave all of that mess alone?"

"You already know the answer to that."

"Even if that means destroying your life in the process?"

Meat thought about Tasha, the baby, and Brad. He nodded.

From behind, someone said, "I ain't never think I was gonna get out of that muthafucka!"

Meat turned around and saw Boo.

When Boo saw him he said, "We made it up out of that muthafucka!"

Meat nodded.

Boo approached them. "Man, let a nigga get a ride home. I stay right there in Lib."

"You got to ask her; I ain't driving."

Boo looked at Tip and said in a British accent, "Could you be so kind as to transport me home? I assure you that I'm a perfect gentleman."

Tip smiled. "Sure."

They walked to Tip's 2004 Navigator and got in. Boo looked around, admiring the interior. "This bitch is nice."

"Thank you," Tip said awkwardly.

Boo stuck his head between the front seats and extended his hand. "I'm Boo, but my friends call me Boobie Dollars."

Tip shook his hand. "Tip."

When they reached Liberty Street Projects, Boo said, "Make a right in the second parking lot."

Tip turned into the parking lot and passed a woman sitting on a porch.

Boo's attention shifted to the woman. "Ole Erica. Ever since that nigga Manus been home, she don't want to give a nigga none."

Meat snapped around. "Who you say?"

"Erica."

"Nah, the other name."

"Manus. That's her baby's daddy."

"He's tall with corn rows?"

"Yeah. His uncle got that detail shop on Chapel Hill Boulevard..." Then he said to Tip, "Stop right here."

Tip stopped the SUV.

Boo said, "Thank you."

"No problem."

"No problem? Well, can you come pick me up in the morning and take me to work?"

"Uh ..."

"I'm just playing," Boo said, laughing. "But y'all take it easy."

"You too."

As he got out of the truck, Meat called him.

"What's up?"

"Is that where she lives?"

Boo looked from Meat to Tip, then back to Meat. "Yeah. You want me to hook you up? Man, she does this trick with ice that —"

"Nah, nah," Meat said, cutting him off. "It ain't nothing like that. I'll see you around."

*　　　*　　　*

Twenty minutes later, a Range Rover pulled up at Erica's place. Manus looked over at Lil' Charles. "I'll see you next weekend, okay?"

"Okay. Don't forget to feed my fish."

"I'm not. You got your asthma pump, right?"

Lil' Charles looked in the outer pocket of his book bag and saw the pump. "Yeah, I got it."

"Okay. Tell your sister I said hey."

"Okay." Lil' Charles got out of the truck and ran to his mother, who was sitting on the porch. As Manus pulled off, he glanced at Erica.

She held up four fingers, indicating that he had four days left to get the money.

Butterflies fluttered in Manus' stomach. Not only was his situation with Erica causing it, but yesterday's incident played a bigger part.

Since yesterday, his mind and heart had been pacing a mile each second. The shooting had been on the news constantly. The police still hadn't identified the bodies of L and Amado. Each time the story aired, Manus expected to hear something about himself or the description of his car. It was a good thing that he had kept a spare key to Grip's Range Rover. What baffled him most was the fact that

Meat's face and the site where he had crashed were also all over the news. Manus knew that he had to straighten his differences with Meat before something tragic happened. He hoped Lauren had gotten through to Meat.

He drove aimlessly.

*　　　*　　　*

Tasha opened her eyes for a few seconds before closing them again. For a brief second, she saw her mother beside her. When she opened them again, in what she assumed to be a few seconds later, her mother was asleep on a nearby Lazy Boy. Her thoughts were distorted from the anesthetics. It took her a moment to get it together. When she did, her hands shot down to her stomach. When she discovered that it was flat, she began screaming.

*　　　*　　　*

Tip pulled up at Meat's apartment. He jumped out.

Tip jumped out behind him, calling his name.

"What?" he snapped.

"What are you about to do?"

Meat let himself into his apartment and went straight to his bedroom closet.

Tip repeated herself.

"I'm about to finish what they started."

Being an innocent victim herself, she said, "Please don't involve that woman. She don't got nothing to do with none of that stuff."

Meat spun around with a mask of fury on his face. "Neither did Tasha or my baby, but look at them!" He turned around to the closet and pulled out a wad of money from a coat pocket. "Here, man," he said, shoving the money in her hands. "Thanks for bailing me out. I'll holla at you."

Tip slung the money to the floor. "I don't care about no money. I care about you! Why can't you see that?"

Meat ignored her and turned back to the closet. He reached on the top shelf and grabbed a black case. As he turned to leave the room, Tip stepped in front of him and blocked his path. "I can't let you throw away your life."

"A'ight now. You better move."

"You might get killed if you go over there."

"They might come kill me if I don't."

"Please, Meat!" she pleaded. "You're only thinking about yourself, and I couldn't take it if something happened to you."

Meat took a deep breath and exhaled. "It's like this, Tip. You're cool with me, but I doubt if it'll ever exceed past that. I don't need you; I don't want you. The best thing that you can do is pick that money up and go on about your business."

Tip had a look in her eyes of helplessness. She then looked at the money on the floor.

Meat brushed past her and headed out the door.

CHAPTER 26

Erica dialed Manus' number and it rang three times before he answered.

"Yeah?"

"Manus. I need for you to come take me to the hospital."

Manus sucked his teeth. He couldn't believe the nerve of her to ask him for a favor. "To the hospital for what?"

"Lil' Charles is sick. He just had an asthma attack."

"What? Call an ambulance and I'll meet y'all at the hospital," he said frantically.

"Uh, it's not that serious. He's just wheezing now. I just want to check him in so he can get a breathing treatment."

"A'ight. I'll be there in ten minutes."

"Okay, hurry."

Erica hung up the phone and looked up at the gunman. "He's on the way."

The man lowered the gun from her head. "Good job."

*   *   *

"Calm down, baby," Tasha's mother said.

"My baby! My baby!"

Tasha's mother continued to try to calm her down, but her efforts were to no avail. Realizing that it was out of her control, she pressed the nurse's button.

Fifteen seconds later, a nurse entered the room and rushed to the bedside. When talking wouldn't calm Tasha down, the nurse called the doctor.

The doctor entered the room and injected a mild sedative into her I.V.

Tasha gradually calmed down. "My ... baby."

The doctor grabbed her hand. "We're doing everything we can to save him. Luckily the bullet missed him."

On her side, Tasha looked at the doctor with surprise. "My ... baby's ... still alive?"

Tasha's mother said, "That's right, baby. He's just premature."

The doctor said, "Now rest. We need you healthy."

"Call ... Meat, Momma."

"His mother called here and ..."

Tasha slipped out of consciousness before her mother could finish the sentence.

*   *   *

Manus pulled up at Erica's apartment complex and jumped out of the truck. When he got on the porch he saw, through the screen door, that the door was slightly ajar. "Erica."

"Come in, it's open."

Manus entered the apartment. When he was halfway through the kitchen, he heard a noise behind him. Before he could turn around, a blow to the head sent him into blackness.

*   *   *

In his Maxima, Meat realized the mistake that he'd made yesterday. He knew that he had let his emotions get the best of him. But today was different. He wasn't going to settle for a cheap thrill. His eyes were on the prize.

*   *   *

A brutal smack to the face woke Manus out of his slumber. When his eyes focused, he saw an unfamiliar man with dreads standing over him.

Dread smiled and said, "You're a hard nigga to catch up with."

"What the fuck?" Manus said as he sat up.

"Daddy!"

Manus looked to his right and saw Erica and the kids bunched together on the couch. Both kids were visibly frightened. "Everything's gonna be cool. Don't worry," Manus said, trying to console them.

Erica said, "I'm sorry. He made me call you."

Manus looked back at Dread, "What's going on? Do I know you?"

"Nah, but you know my mans."

"Who's your mans?"

"You'll see. We're about to take a lil' ride."

"You got *me* now. Leave them out of it."

"Nah, they're my insurance that you won't try nothing crazy."

Manus shook his head. "I can't agree to that. You got to compromise some."

"I don't got to do shit. I'm the one with the gun!"

"Look —"

Dread suddenly smacked Manus in the head with the gun.

The kids began to scream.

"You think this is a game? You think I won't knock your brains out like I did Brad?" Dread saw the look on Manus' face then grabbed Lil' Charles off the couch. He put the gun to his head. "Go 'head. Try something, and you will be responsible."

Kandis was crying at the top of her lungs.

Dread spun to Erica and pointed his gun at Kandis. "Shut that lil' bitch up before I do!"

Erica grabbed Kandis and buried her face in her bosom. "Why are you doing this, Dread?"

"For the same reason you be fucking everything. Money." He turned back to Manus. "Now stand the fuck up."

Manus got up slowly. "Just tell me who's paying you to do this."

"You'll see soon enough." He motioned for Erica to stand up, too. "Now, we gonna walk real easy-like to my car. If anyone so much as stumbles, I'll push this lil' boy's shit back."

For the first time, Lil' Charles began to cry. Manus said, "Everything's gonna be a'ight. Don't cry."

Dread tossed Manus a set of car keys. "Go to the red Chrysler. You're driving." They filed out of the apartment, Dread trailing with Lil' Charles. Dread put on a toboggan and pulled it low over his brows. As soon as they were a few feet from the car, Manus heard a car door open. He looked up and saw Meat.

*   *   *

Shawnda drove to Erica's house blasting and singing her favorite song, "I used to be scared of the dick; now I throw lips to the shit, handle it like a real bitch ..."

All night she had been thinking about Dread's phone conversation that had been in the bathroom. No matter how much she had tried to dismiss it as harmless, everything in her soul told her that it was something much more.

She sped toward Erica's house. She had to warn Manus.

*   *   *

Meat pulled into the parking lot. Before he put the car in park, he spotted Manus and some other people coming out of the apartment. With the mini-M-16 already out of its case, Meat got out of the car and cocked it.

*   *   *

When Dread saw the man get out of the car and cock some sort of machine gun, he instantly raised his gun and began firing.

Lil' Charles took advantage of the diversion and ran away from Dread.

Meat returned fire.

Manus dove to the ground and tucked his head.

As fast as the shooting began, it had stopped.

When Manus looked up, he saw Dread lowering his smoking gun. Manus then looked in Meat's direction and saw him on the ground motionless.

Dread saw Erica and her kids forty yards away, running in the opposite direction. Neighbors could be seen looking out their windows and screen doors.

Dread knew that his plan was now ruined, but he couldn't let Manus off the hook that easily. He focused on Manus again and aimed his gun.

*　　　*　　　*

Shawnda turned into Erica's parking lot just as the shootout erupted. She saw Erica and the kids running in the opposite direction. When the man turned and pointed a gun at Manus, Shawnda instantly recognized the all-black Versace jacket that he wore.

She stomped on the accelerator and raced straight for Dread.

By the time Dread looked back and saw the car, it was three feet away. The impact of the collision threw Dread ten feet in the air, and he landed fifteen feet away with a hard thud.

Shawnda threw her car in park and got out. "Manus, you okay?"

Manus got to his feet. "Yeah, thanks."

She nodded and looked at Dread.

Manus walked over to Dread and saw that his legs were twisted in an awkward position. He crouched down. "Who sent you to do this?"

Through clenched teeth, Dread said, "Fuck you, nigga. Kill me!"

Manus retrieved Dread's gun, which lay a few feet away, and aimed it at Dread.

"No, Manus. He ain't worth it."

Dread said, "Either way, I win. 'Cause my man still gonna hunt you down and kill you, so you might as well get your issue in before my mans get his."

Manus pondered on that for a second before he set the pistol down. Then he lifted one of Dread's broken legs and stomped it at the knee. The sound of a bone cracking could not be heard over Dread's scream. Shawnda turned her back and forced the vomit back down.

When Manus lifted Dread's other leg, Dread began to plead. "Please!"

"Then you better tell me who sent you."

When Dread hesitated, Manus raised his foot.

"A'ight, a'ight! I'll tell you!"

*　　　*　　　*

After getting Erica to call an ambulance, Manus walked over to Meat. He lay in a pool of blood with his eyes flickering. Manus grabbed his hand. "Hold on, rap. Help is on the way." He then picked up the mini-

M-16 and got into the Range Rover.

Lil' Charles ran to the truck and knocked on the window.

Manus rolled down the window. "Stay with your mom."

"Daddy, please don't go and get in trouble."

"I'm not. I'll be back later."

"Then let me go with you."

"No, you can't. But I promise I'll be back."

"You got to promise that you won't go to jail first."

This caught Manus off guard, and his hesitation caused Lil' Charles to frown. To ease his worries, Manus leaned out of the window and kissed him on the forehead. "I promise." And with that said, Manus put the truck in reverse.

*   *   *

The house sat in the southern part of Durham, in a neighborhood called Greenwood. When Manus pulled up, he saw a BMW and a Jaguar in the driveway. He got out and looked inside both cars.

Manus crept to the side of the house and looked through each window. Although each room was lavish, the last room took his breath. The room contained a large safe that sat open. From what he could see, it appeared to be filled with money.

The backyard was fenced in by a ten-foot wooden fence. Manus strapped the assault rifle over his shoulder and cautiously climbed the fence. When he landed, he was rushed by a fifty-pound buckskin boxer.

*   *   *

Dread lay on the ground in frustration and agony. Not only was the kidnapping and shooting charge going to put him away for a long time, but he knew that the murder of Brad alone would get him life. He silently chastised himself for openly admitting to the murder. Erica was sure to tell the police after what he had put her through.

An ambulance and two police cruisers arrived at the same time and rushed to his and Meat's aid.

One officer stood back and listened as Erica told him her

version of what had happened.

Dread closed his eyes as the paramedic and officer approached him. As soon as the paramedic bent down to check for a pulse, Dread brought the pocketknife out of his pocket and started stabbing the man in the neck.

The officer reacted swiftly and fired two shots at Dread.

Dread went limp and stared at the sky with a gaping hole in his forehead.

*   *   *

Manus' first instinct was to swing the assault rifle around and kill the dog, but when he saw its stubby tail wagging, he relaxed and scratched the dog behind the ears.

"Where's your master at?" Manus whispered.

As if understanding the question, the dog turned around and led the way. Manus followed the dog with the assault rifle extended. The dog stopped at the corner of the house and looked back at Manus. Manus put his back to the wall and took a deep breath. In a swift motion, he swung the rifle around the corner and kept creeping.

Next to the pool, Tory sat at a table snorting cocaine. When he looked up and saw Manus, he dropped the rolled-up bill on the table. The men locked eyes for a moment before Tory shifted his eyes to the dog. He casually picked up a champagne glass and took a sip. "I never did like that mutt." Then he threw the glass at the dog.

The boxer dodged the glass and growled at Tory.

"So Dread sold me out, huh?"

Ignoring the question, Manus said, "Why did you have Brad killed? He ain't have nothing to do with what I did to you."

"For one, fuck Brad. For two, he had everything to do with it when he stuck his nose in it in prison."

"You know what goes around comes around."

Tory wheeled himself around the table so that Manus could see the wheelchair. "So when this gonna come around to you? I was minding my goddamn business when you came and fucked my life up!"

Manus observed that Tory was only wearing a robe with some boxers on. His upper body was ripped with muscles, but his legs looked like they belonged to a twelve- year-old.

"As you can see," Tory said, gesturing to the bottles of champagne on the table, "I was going to have a going-away party for you today. The same kind of party I had the night Brad was killed."

Manus aimed the weapon at Tory's face, but Tory showed no type of fear. His eyes seemed to beg Manus to pull the trigger. Removing his finger from the trigger, Manus thought about his reason for being there. The plan had been simple. Avenge Brad's death. He thought about what Lil' Charles had asked of him. Second thoughts now settled in like morning fog on a prison yard. But through all of this, he knew that Tory wouldn't give up until one of them was dead.

Tory took advantage of Manus' daze and slipped his hand on the palm-sized .45 in the pocket of his robe. In a quick motion, he drew the gun and pulled the trigger. Nothing happened. He had forgotten to take the safety off. But before Tory could do anything else, Manus smashed him in the face with the butt of the assault rifle. The blow knocked the man unconscious and sent him rolling backwards and into the pool.

Manus watched as Tory floated face down in the water. He watched for a few minutes before heading for the most expensive room of the house.

CHAPTER 27

Charles Sr. woke up and smiled at the ceiling. He felt good. He and Erica had had a long discussion last night about their future together, and had come to agreeable terms. For the first time since the beginning of their relationship, they had made love all night. The way Erica had performed oral sex on him, Charles knew it had to be love.

He had decided at that very moment that it didn't matter that Lil' Charles wasn't his. They were still young and had plenty of time to make other babies. And with Lil' Charles living with Manus now, his relationship with Erica had improved over the past two weeks.

Charles reached on the nightstand and grabbed his Newports. He saw Kandis walk into the room, rubbing sleep out of her eyes.

She got on the bed and put her head on his chest. Charles looked at his beautiful daughter, who was the spitting image of her mother.

"Good morning, baby."

"Morning, daddy."

"You just waking up?"

"Uhm hmm. I want some cereal."

"Why you ain't get your momma to fix you some pancakes or something?"

"'Cause she ain't here."

Charles then remembered that it was the first of the month. Erica always got up early to cash her check and get her hair and nails taken care of. He got up. "Come on, baby."

They entered the kitchen and Charles grabbed a box of Cinnamon Toast Crunch from the top of the refrigerator. He noticed a note taped to the box and read it.

Charles:

> I hate to do it this way, but I know that if I would have told you face to face, you would have tried to stop me. It's easier this way. In the last few weeks or so, I've realized that life is too short to be unhappy. I feel trapped with you and the kids. Y'all came into my life before I got the chance to live my own. I'm leaving Kandis with you. You are her father, and I trust that you will take care of her to the best of your ability. It's useless trying to find me, so don't waste your time.

Love always,
Erica

P.S. I swear I didn't leave you for another man, so don't be mad.

Charles let out a scream and slammed the box of cereal on the floor.

*   *   *

Manus' brand new Infinity pulled up at the beaten-down duplex. Gee said, "Are you sure this is the place? You said you only been here once."

"I think so." Manus got out of the car and smiled at Lil' Charles in the back seat.

A minute after knocking at the door, a woman yelled, "Who is it?"

"It's Manus. Is Mrs. Beasley here?"

An older lady with reddish hair stood behind the screen door. "Yes? I'm she."

"Uh, I don't know if you remember me, but I came here with L once."

The lady put on her glasses. "Yes, I remember you. I have the memory of an elephant. Mind you that my memory is the only thing that isn't fading."

Manus smiled. Then she said, "How come I didn't see you at

Lamont's wake or funeral?"

"For various reasons. But the main one is I'm not too big on things like that."

"I understand. Most people ain't."

"I'm sorry about L, though."

"I am too. Lamont may have done some evil things, but he wasn't a bad person."

"I know. But Mrs. Beasley, L gave me something to give to you. Hold up … it's in the car."

He walked back to the car and asked Gee to press the trunk release button.

He carried a duffel bag to the porch.

Mrs. Beasley said, "Is that some of Lamont's clothes?"

"No, Mrs. Beasley. I think we better go in the house with this."

Mrs. Beasley unlocked the screen door and held it open for him.

Manus set the bag in the chair and gestured toward it.

Mrs. Beasley opened it. When she saw the contents, she said, "Lordy Jesus!"

"L told me to tell you that he loves you, and to not cry for him."

Mrs. Beasley put her hand over her mouth. "Were you there when he died?"

Manus looked away. "Please don't make me lie to you."

"Did you kill him?"

"No, Mrs. Beasley. The guy they found with him did. I was just a friend."

"I sense that you are. Shoot, Lord knows you are, or you wouldn't have brought this money to me. I tell you, God works in mysterious ways. My Social Security check got stolen, my bills are due, and I didn't know how I was gonna pay my bills."

"Well, Mrs. Beasley, I have to go. Take care, and be careful with that money."

"I will, and God bless you."

*　　　*　　　*

Manus rode in silence as Gee and Lil' Charles conversed.

When he turned into a community and stopped at an apartment, Gee said, "What now?"

"I'll be right back."

"Hurry up, baby. I want to be on time."

Lil' Charles said, "Yeah, daddy. We got to be on time."

"We will." Then he looked back at Gee. "You rubbing off on him."

Gee shrugged and smiled.

Manus got out of the car and walked to the apartment. He knocked and waited.

"Who is it?"

"It's Manus." When the door opened, he saw the woman and smiled. "What's up, Tasha?"

"Nothing … No, Cocoa," She said, blocking the door with her leg so the buckskin boxer couldn't get out.

Manus stepped in and bent down to scratch the dog behind his ears. "Hey, boy, with your fat stomach."

"That rascal eats everything but his dog food."

Manus stood again. "How's your back?"

"It aches from time to time, but it's coming along."

"What about the baby?"

"Greedy."

"Can you blame him? He's trying to get his weight up." They laughed.

"Have a seat. I'll go get Meat." Tasha disappeared in the back.

Moments later, Meat came up the hallway moving like an old man. His neck was bandaged, and a bulge above his hip was visible.

Manus met him. "What's up?"

"Shit," Meat said in a raspy voice. The men bumped fists.

"How you feeling?"

"Like a lead magnet."

"I just came to see how you were doing."

"Other than this disgusting-ass shit bag," he said, looking down at the bulge, "I'm cool."

"How's Tasha taking Gloria's death?"

"She cries sometimes, but I think she's taking it well."

"Word."

"I just got off the phone with Lauren and Bobby, and they want us to come over for dinner next Sunday."

"That's word. You know I'm with that. Oh, Grip said you playing sick just so you won't have to take that fishing trip with us."

Meat laughed. "Never that. Him and Six called us out, so I got to go. Tell him I said give me another week, and I'll be ready."

"Word."

"Want some breakfast?"

"Nah, I got to go. Gee and Charles is in the car."

"Oh. Tell them I said what's up."

"Word. But I'll hit you later."

The men bumped fists again then Manus turned to leave.

Meat said, "Yo."

"What's up?" Manus asked, turning back around.

"I know that I already apologized, but —"

"You straight," he said, cutting him off.

"I know, but check. I came so close to doing some bullshit that it ain't funny."

"It's gravy. If anything, I feel like all of this shit is my fault. If I wouldn't have robbed Tory, none of this shit would've happened."

"Don't be so hard on yourself. If Brad would've known the outcome of helping you, he still would've done the same thing."

"Yeah, he was real like that."

Manus lightly slapped Meat on the back. "Hurry up and get healthy. I got a business proposition for you. You'll be rich in no time."

"That's what I'm talking about."

*   *   *

An obese white man walked inside the building and took the elevator to the twelfth floor. When he got off, his secretary looked up from what she was doing.

"Good morning, Mr. Rich."

"Good morning, Nancy. How are you feeling this morning?"

"I would complain, but it wouldn't do any good."

"No, it wouldn't."

"I put the Barson file on your desk and you have a nine o'clock appointment with Mrs. Applewhite."

"Yes, I remember."

As Jesse Rich headed toward his office, Nancy said, "Oh ... Mr. Rich?"

"Yes?" he said turning around.

"I also put a package on your desk; it came in about ten minutes ago."

"Thank you. And can you bring me some coffee?"

"Sure," she said, getting up from her desk.

Jesse Rich entered his office and stopped at the package. He opened it and discovered an envelope and a letter. After reading the letter, Jesse Rich opened the envelope and pulled out a check.

"Here's your coffee, Mr. Rich," Nancy said, coming through the door.

Jesse took the coffee and said, "Hold on for a second." He sat the coffee down and went through his Rolodex to find a phone number. Pulling one section out, he said, "Call a Mrs. Williams and tell her I received the fee and that I'm starting Pat's case immediately."

*   *   *

Thirty minutes later, Manus pulled into the large parking lot and they got out of the car.

Gee looked at him. "You look nervous."

"I am, a lil' bit. It's been a minute since I've seen her."

"Everything is going to be just fine. You'll see."

Manus hugged her. "What would I do with out you?"

"Let's not think like that."

They kissed, and Lil' Charles said, "Ughh!" They all laughed and walked toward the Women's State Prison.

228

LOST AND FOUND

Born August 6, 1977 to single parent, Jacqueline Bullock, Kevin Bullock was always bright and spontaneous. Raised in the slums of Durham, North Carolina, he experienced life at it's worst and knew that he wanted better for his children. Like a lot of black males from the slums, he became mesmerized with street life and as a result soon found himself in and out of jail. Being a single parent and unable to find a suitable job because of the felonies on his record, he struggled to balance his street life during the day while his son was at daycare with being an attentive father at night. Soon, his street life got the best of him and he found himself locked up in federal prison with a fifteen year sentence.

More depressed because he felt like he had failed his children, he began to vent out on paper to maintain his sanity. When a fellow inmate read his stories, he encouraged Kevin to submit them to a publisher. He thought that Kevin's work was just as good, if not better, than the urban books that were floating around. When the idea of being able to support his family from prison dawned on him, Kevin began to write feverishly.

A year later, he signed a two book deal with Urban Lifestyle Press.

Other titles available from
Urban Lifestyle Press...

Name: _____

Address: _____

City/State: _____

Zip: _____

	TITLES	PRICES
	Entangled	$13.95
	Fetish	$14.95
	Tennis Shoe Pimp	$14.95
	Street Fame	$14.95

FREE SHIPPING

TOTAL $_____

To order online visit
www.beststreetfiction.com

Mail orders please send cashiers check or money order to:
P.O. Box 12714 • Charlotte, NC 28220

Other titles available from
Urban Lifestyle Press...

To order online visit
www.beststreetfiction.com

Mail orders please send cashiers check or money order to:
P.O. Box 12714 • Charlotte, NC 28220